FORBIDDEN
Love

FORBIDDEN Love

RHAYNE

Autumn

"Wait! Wait!" I yelled as I held my plane ticket in the air while running towards the desk clerk. They had just announced the last call for all passengers boarding the flight to Chicago, and there was no way I was missing that flight. McKenzie had called me and told me Mercedes was in labor, and I wanted to be there for the birth of my little brother or sister. Although Mercedes and McKenzie weren't my birth parents, they were my family, and they have treated me as such since I came into their lives. You see, McKenzie was married to my mother, Sharon, for five years. He had no idea I existed until I showed up on his doorstep the day of my mother's funeral. Mercedes was my mom's best friend, who ended up with McKenzie, after they discovered both her boyfriend and my mom were having an affair with the same man. Yep, that's right, the same man. They had some Jerry Springer shit going on.

After putting my luggage in the carrier above my seat, I quickly sat down. I had already caused a ruckus and was embarrassed, to say the least.

"What a way to make an entrance," a deep voice stated.

I turned to see the face that went with the voice and looked into the most beautiful pair of brown eyes staring back at me. Usually, I wasn't at a loss for words. But at that moment, I felt self-conscious and couldn't speak. I cursed at myself for not taking the time to do my hair or put on make-up. I had pulled my hair back into a ponytail and put on a baseball cap. Deciding I was going to sleep most of the way, I opted not to put on any make-up, and boy was that a bad mistake.

He smiled, showcasing his dimples and perfectly aligned teeth.

"Cat got your tongue?" He asked, jokingly.

"No, but you can," I said in a shallow voice.

He leaned in closer. "I'm sorry, I didn't hear you."

I inhaled the scent of his cologne. The masculine fragrance of sandalwood was intoxicating and had me on a journey of lust. His arm brushed against mine, and I refocused my thoughts.

"I said, yeah, you're telling me."

He smiled as he held his hand out. "I'm Antwan."

"Autumn." I took hold of his hand, and we exchanged a quick handshake.

"So, why are you going to Chicago?" He asked.

"My mom's friend is having a baby. She's in labor as we speak."

"Oh, that's cool."

"And why are you traveling to Chicago?" I inquired.

"I'm a journalist. I'm working on a story."

"What story?"

"It's on the attempted murder of the CEO of Princeton Enterprises."

"Oh, I heard about that. His name was Byron Jefferson, right?"

I already knew the story; after all, my mom was involved in it. Byron was her lover and her downfall.

"Yes." He nodded. "Well, they have caught the guy that did it, and I am doing an exclusive on him."

"Awesome. Hopefully, you can get the truth."

"I always do. Believe that." He winked.

I opened my purse and took out lipstick and a small mirror. My Aunt Mattie always said a little lipstick could work wonders when you're not wearing make-up.

"You don't need that," Antwan said.

"Oh, yes, I do."

"No, you don't. You are beautiful just the way you are." He smiled. "Besides, I like your natural beauty."

"Thank you, but you don't know these lips like I do."

"I would like to," he interrupted.

Blood filled my cheeks, and I started to blush. I put away my items and cocked my head to the side.

"Maybe, you will," I smiled.

Antwan and I talked the entire four-hour flight. You would have thought we had known each other all our lives. We exchanged phone numbers and discussed getting together for dinner before he left for LA.

Once we landed in Chicago, I rented a car and went straight to the hospital from the airport. When I opened the door to Mercedes' room, McKenzie and her parents were there. McKenzie stood to give me a hug. Although happy to see me, it was apparent Mercedes was having some discomfort. I walked over to the bed and gave her a hug.

"Can I get you anything?" I asked.

"Yeah, get this baby out of here." She touched her protruding belly and chuckled.

I made a sad face. "I'm afraid that's out of my hands."

"One can only wish. Whew, another contraction." She frowned.

"It will be over soon, honey," McKenzie said, trying to comfort her. That must have been the wrong thing to say because she gave him a look that said, 'You can go to hell.'

"Well on that note, I'm going to go get me a cup of coffee. Would any of you like something?" He wrote down everyone's order. "Come walk with me, sunshine," he said to me as he started to leave. I nodded and walked out behind him.

"So, how is LA treating you?"

"It's fine. I don't have time to do much. It seems like all I do is go to school, work, and study."

"Oh, yeah, I remember those days," he mused. Where are you working again?"

"I'm working at Belinda's Hair Salon as her shampoo girl," I lied.

There was no way I was telling McKenzie I had taken over my cousin Destini's phone sex company. He and Mercedes thought I was attending college in LA because I wanted a change. But the truth is, when Destini ended up in jail for trying to have Chloe murdered, she asked me to take over her business-FANTASY. And it had proven to be more than I really wanted to deal with.

"Right." He nodded. "Well, you just keep doing what you're doing, and it will all pay off in the long run." He wrapped his arm around my shoulders. "I'm proud of you, Autumn. You know, that right?"

"Of course," I smiled.

I told McKenzie about my conversation with Antwan on the flight and that he was doing a cover story about Byron Jefferson. He wasn't all that enthused but looked forward to reading the story. He had some questions, and maybe through the article, he would get the answers he needed.

Twelve hours after my arrival, McKenzie Jr. was born. He weighed eight pounds ten ounces and had the chubbiest little cheeks. I witnessed the birth, and it was an amazing experience to see MJ enter the world. When I held him in my arms for the first time, I was overwhelmed with emotion. As his little fingers wrapped around my pinky finger, I promised him that I would always be there for him, no matter what. I was his big sister for life, and I loved him so much already.

Although, my visit to Chicago was great, it was time for me to return to LA. While sitting on the plane waiting for takeoff, I thought about Antwan. We never got together before he left. *Maybe it wasn't meant to be.*

When we landed at the airport, Zora was waiting for me. She had been my right-hand ever since I took over Fantasy. I met her in Belinda's salon at the right time. She needed a job, and I needed a phone sex operator. I also hired Gina and David as operators, and Anna stayed on part-time as one. I, on the other hand, took on the role of receptionist after I fired Chloe. Although Chloe hadn't done anything wrong, I felt it was best due to the way things went down between her and Destini.

"Hey, girl. Welcome back," she said, giving me a hug.

"Thanks. But I could have used another week," I said, hugging her back. She took my handbag while I pulled the suitcase on wheels behind me.

"How have things been?" I asked.

She smiled. "Like a smooth-running machine."

"Thanks for keeping an eye on things for me."

"No problem. Oh, there is one thing you should know."

"What's that?"

"Ty came over and beat the hell out of Anna."

"What!" I was shocked. I had never heard of him putting his hands-on, Anna, before. "Well, I hope she locked him up."

"No, she didn't. But I had his ass locked up. Teach him not to put his damn hands on her, at least not around me," she said matter-of-factly.

"Good. Did Anna say what started it?"

"No. She won't talk about it."

"Okay, I'll talk to her later. In the meantime, I just want to get a shower and relax for the rest of the evening."

It was always something about Ty I didn't like, but I couldn't put my finger on it. I met him a year ago at FANTASY when I visited Destini during my summer break from school. He worked there as an operator, and he had this, 'I'm God's gift to women' attitude. That was a big turn off to me. But Anna, she loved him, and there wasn't anything or anyone that could change her mind about him. Now granted, he was very handsome, with his pretty green eyes and curly hair. He looked like a younger Michael Ealy to me. But I don't care how good-looking or attractive a guy was, if he put his hands on a woman, then he is nothing but a low life punk to me. I don't do women beaters, and that will not be tolerated at FANTASY. As far as I'm concerned, Anna needs to kick his ass to the curb, and I will let her know just how I feel about it when I see her.

Anna

I stood in the parking lot of the county jail, waiting on Ty to come out of the building. He had spent a week in jail for beating me up, and I was reminded of that beating every time I looked in the mirror and saw my black eye. This was his first time beating me, and it was going to be his last. I purchased a 22-caliber handgun, and I swore I would shoot his ass dead if he ever laid another hand on me. Why I let him get away with it this time, you ask? Well, because I was not going to let him come between me and my money.

Ty walked out of the building with his chest all poked out with pride. I smiled. Aww, look at you. You think you're macho now, but you're a dead man walking, I thought as I returned the hug, he gave me.

"Hey, Babe. You miss me?" He asked so arrogantly.

"Of course," I said, stroking his ego.

"Good. I'm a tap that ass when we get to my place."

He walked around to the passenger side of the car and got in.

"We have to make a drop," I said, putting on my seatbelt before backing out of the parking space.

"Where's the drop?"

"At Victor Heights. Geno is meeting us there."

He nodded his head and turned the radio up. The ride was quiet, outside of the loud music blaring. When I drove into the Heights apartment complex, I spotted Geno sitting on the steps as I pulled up to his building. I grabbed the brown paper bag from under the seat and put it in my large handbag. When I got out of the car, he stood up and walked inside the apartment. I followed him. Once inside, I gave him the product, and he gave me the cash. After making sure everything was right, I put the money in my purse.

"Geno, can I use your bathroom before I go? I asked.

"Yeah, first door on the right," he said, clearing the table.

I nodded and headed down the hall.

His bathroom looked just as I expected. The beige walls were bare, except for a small black clock on the wall over the towel holder. The shower curtain was blue, and there were two matching blue rugs on the floor.

I took a sanitary pad from my purse and smeared the ketchup from the two packets I had taken off

Geno's table on it. I really didn't care two fucks about having sex with Ty. He was a sorry lay, and on top of that, he was a selfish one, too. I pulled some tissue off the roller, wrapped the packets and pad wrapper into it, and threw it in the small wicker basket next to the toilet.

When I came out of the bathroom, Geno was still sitting at the table.

"Nice doing business with you," I said, before leaving.

When I got back in the car, Ty started tripping.

"What took you so damn long?" He snapped.

"Ty, I wasn't in there that long. He tried the product and then counted out the money. That's all."

He looked at me sideways. "Um, hmm. Don't let me find out you're fucking him. I'mma kill both of you."

"I'm not," I said, starting the car. I really didn't know where all this attitude was coming from. He went from being loving to being cruel. I put the gear in drive and drove him home. When we arrived at his apartment, I didn't turn the car off.

"What you doing? You're not coming in?"

"No, I have to get back to Fantasy. My shift is starting."

"Well, come break a brother off before you go."

"Can't. I'm on my period."

"You're lying," he contested.

I pulled down my pants and showed him the pad.

"Alright, I'll holler at you later." He kissed me on the cheek and got out of the car.

When I drove away, I shook my head in disgust. One thing I've learned about Ty, when I'm on my period, he acts like it's a plague and doesn't want anything to do with me, physically or affectionately which is fine by me; no love lost here. If it wasn't for our hustle, I would've been cut him loose.

I stopped by Chloe and Devin's place on my way home to say hello. I hadn't seen either one of them since my fight with Ty.

Shortly after I rang the doorbell, Chloe answered.

"Hey, Saucy," she teased.

"Hey, Chloe."

"How have you been? You're looking much better," she said, referring to the fading bruises on my face.

"Yeah." I shook my head at the thought of the beating. "I'm making it. I just picked him up from the jail and took him home."

"Anna, we have to talk about what happened."

"I know," I sighed.

She nodded. "Well, I think you should get rid of him. He's going to do it again, you know."

"And that will be his last time," I said, looking her right in the eyes so that she was clear that I meant what I said.

"Don't do anything that will get you in trouble. He's not worth it."

"Um, hmm. Well, as long as Ty doesn't put his hands on me, he has nothing to worry about. But if he does, it will be his last breath, and that's a promise."

"Okay. Well, I'm going to leave that alone. You are grown, and I can't tell you what to do," she shrugged. "Come on. The group is out back." She walked towards the back door, and I followed behind her.

"You are welcome to join us for dinner," she said as we walked through the kitchen and out the back door. Devin, Ricky, and Belinda were sitting around the table on the patio eating.

"Hello, everyone," I said, taking notice that they were all looking at my eye. At least that's how I felt.

"Hi, Anna." Devin gave me a hug.

"Hey." Belinda and Ricky followed suit. We engaged in small talk for a little while, then I said my goodbyes and left.

Belinda

Just as Anna was driving off, I walked in the living room where Chloe was standing at the front door, waving goodbye to her.

"Girl, you know they say he's pimping her, right?" I commented.

Chloe turned around to face me. "Who's pimping her?" She looked bewildered.

"Ty."

"Ty! Girl, Ty ain't no pimp." She walked past me and into the kitchen.

"Well, I'm telling you what the streets are saying?

"Well, the streets are lying, and I don't want to hear another word about what the streets are saying. Anna is my friend. Trust me. If Ty was trying to pimp her, she would have come to Devin and me about it."

"Well, did she come to you about that ass-whipping he put on her last week, or did you have to hear that from me?" I folded my arms. "I'll wait."

She grabbed the bread off of the counter and put it in the refrigerator. "Okay, I'll give you that one, but I know her well enough to know she's not out there selling herself."

"We'll see. The truth always has a way of coming to light." I shrugged.

"Yeah, it does."

We walked back outside to where the men were still sitting at the table talking.

"Hey babe, you two, alright?" Ricky asked, looking back and forth between Chloe and me.

"Yeah, we're fine," I said, taking a seat next to him. Chloe sat down next to Devin, but she didn't say anything.

I know they felt it because the tension between us was so thick you could cut it with a knife.

"Hey, man. It's been good. We are going to get on out of here," Ricky said, standing to leave. He and Devin shook hands. "I'll call you tomorrow." Chloe stood, and he hugged her.

I gave Devin a hug, and Chloe and I just looked at each other.

"I'll talk to you later, Chloe," I said, walking towards the door. She didn't respond.

Once we pulled out of the driveway, Ricky asked, "What the hell just happened back there?"

"She got pissed off because I told her the word on the street is that Anna is being pimped by Ty."

"Why would you tell her that? You don't know if that shit is true or not. I done told you about running your mouth."

"I thought I could share that info with her. You know, one friend to another. After all, Anna is her girl."

"Belinda, that shit isn't cool. Stay out of people's business and stop gossiping!" He said, putting emphasis on 'gossiping.'

"Yeah, yeah." I turned and looked out of the window. I was done with the conversation. I was only trying to be a friend to Chloe, but from now on, I would keep my damn mouth shut when it came to her precious friend, Anna.

Chloe

Belinda has a way of getting under my skin. If she wasn't married to Ricky, she would be one chick I would never associate with. But, since Ricky and Devin are friends, I have no choice. I will admit that she was the first to tell me about Ty beating Anna. I still don't know how she found that out, but it doesn't surprise me. She's like the president of the street committee. Anyway, by the time I got to Anna, the police were already there. Devin was one of the responding officers on the scene, and he was just about done writing down Anna's account of the fight. Ty, however, was long gone.

"So, what was that all about?" Devin asked after Ricky and Belinda pulled off.

"It's about her running her mouth about shit she doesn't know," I snapped.

He held his hands up. "Whoa! I didn't have anything to do with it."

"I know. I'm sorry. I'm just so pissed right now. Let's talk about it later, okay. I'm going to shower."

"That sounds like a plan." He wrapped his arms around me and gave me a light kiss on the lips. I stepped out of his embrace and walked to the bedroom to get my necessities before heading to the bathroom.

As I stood under the showerhead, enjoying the warm water hitting my skin, Devin joined me. He wrapped his arms around me and began leaving a trail of small kisses down my back. Everything in my core began to stir. He took his foot and slid my left foot over just enough to spread my legs apart, and started caressing my treasure box.

"Mhmm, what are you doing?" I said, as his fingers danced around my clit, making it throb.

He turned me around to face him and took one of my hardened nipples into his mouth. I drew in a deep breath and leaned my head against the shower wall to steady myself. I wrapped my hand around his rod and began teasing its head with my thumb as it continued to grow. Just the feel of his hardness made me wet.

"Aww, you're ready, babe," he said, using his fingers to check the wetness between my thighs.

"Yes." I moaned. He turned me around and entered me from behind, moving slowly at first until my creamy inner hole made it easier to glide in and out with ease. I pushed against his rod with each thrust, causing him to penetrate deeper into my flower.

"That's right babe, give it to me," he said in a low whisper. He pulled my hair, forcing my back to arch and my bottom to poke out as he thrust deeper inside of me. I steadied my legs and tightened the walls of my wetness around his nature. I gyrated my hips in slow motion, taking him all in. "Damn, you feel good."

"Mhmm, so do you, babe."

He was hitting my spot, and I was almost there. He reached around me and massaged my bud with his fingers causing my body to climax; my legs buckled, but he didn't miss a beat. As he approached his own orgasm, he grabbed my hips, and began to move faster, each thrust more intense than the last, until his juices spilled over into my honey cup.

Autumn

I was lying across my bed, staring at the paper with Antwan's phone number on it when I heard a car door shut. I got up and looked out of the window to see who it was; Anna had made it home. So, I went downstairs to talk to her.

"Hey," I said, standing in the doorway of the kitchen as I watched her heat up leftovers in the microwave.

"Hey." She turned around to look at me. Right away, I noticed her black eye.

"So, how are you doing?"

"I'm doing fine, and you?" She responded. Her body language indicated she didn't want to be bothered.

"I'm good. I heard about your fight with Ty."

"I don't want to talk about it."

"Okay, well, I'm just going to say this, and let you be. That right there," I pointed to her eye, "is not cool." She held her head down. "I'm here if you want to talk about it." I turned and walked away.

I was angry at the sight of her face. I wanted to find Ty and whip his ass myself. Only a punk would put his hands on a woman.

I went back upstairs to my room and called Antwan. I needed a distraction, and he would be a good one.

"Hello," a female, on the other end of the phone, answered. I was caught off guard. I didn't know whether to speak or hang up. All kinds of thoughts raced through my head like; Is this his girlfriend or his wife?

"Hello," she repeated.

I decided to take a chance. "Hi, may I speak with Antwan?"

"You have the wrong number," she replied before hanging up. I called the number back.

"Hello," she answered again.

"Hello, I just called you."

"I know," she replied with a hint of agitation in her voice.

"Do you, by any chance, know an Antwan?"

"No, I do not know an Antwan."

"Okay, thanks."

I looked at the phone number again, and just as I was balling up the paper, Anna walked in.

"You have a minute?"

"For you, yes." I smiled. She sat down next to me on the bed.

"Okay, look, I'm not going to sugar coat this thing with Ty. It is what it is. He beat me." She sighed. I didn't say anything, so she went on to explain. "Ty felt I was disrespecting him by talking to this guy at 'Jack of Trades' game room."

"How does talking to someone disrespect him?"

"Well, the guy put his hand on my thigh, and I sort of let it stay there."

"How you sort of let it stay there, Anna?"

"I had been drinking. Ty had gone to the restroom and left me sitting at the bar. This fine brother sat next to me, and we started talking. He offered to buy me a drink, and I gladly accepted it. We were laughing and enjoying each other's company when he moved his hand up my skirt. The next thing I know, Ty was snatching me off the barstool, and forcing me out the building. Once we were inside the car, we began arguing, and he punched me in the eye."

"Did you call the police?" I asked just to see if she would tell me the truth.

"No." She looked down at her feet.

"Why not?"

"Because I felt like it was my fault."

"And how did you come to that conclusion?"

"If I would have told the guy I was not interested. He wouldn't have bought me the drink, and I wouldn't have been entertaining him."

"Anna, it doesn't matter what you did or didn't do, it still does not give Ty the right to put his hands on you," I said sternly. "You do know that, right?"

"Yes, I know." She said, standing to leave. "Thank you for your concern, but I got this, trust me."

"Okay, as I said, I'm here if you need me." I watched as she closed the door behind her. I laid my head on the pillow. Being a boss is not all it's cracked up to be. Dealing with my problems is one thing, but when I have to deal with other people's issues, it's really a headache. I looked over at the crumpled paper I had balled up earlier and tossed it in the small trash basket next to my end table. It's just not meant to be, I thought as I closed my eyes and drifted off to sleep.

Anna

I woke up earlier than usual to go running before starting my shift at Fantasy. I had a lot on my mind, and a good run always seemed to help me clear my head. Today was no exception. By the time I got home, I was feeling great until I walked into my bedroom and found Ty lying across my bed.

"What are you doing here?" I asked, not bothering to hide my annoyance.

He sat up on the bed, "Well, good morning to you, too?"

I rolled my eyes. "What do you want?"

"Oh, so it's like that?"

"What do you want Ty, I have to get ready for my shift."

"I need to borrow your car for a little while."

I walked over to the closet and retrieved the keys from my purse. "Here," I said, handing him the keys. "Be back by three o'clock."

"Yeah." He walked towards the door.

"Ty, I'm serious. I have a three-thirty hair appointment today."

"Ok. I'll be back at three." He tried to kiss me, but I turned my head. "You are tripping." He chuckled and walked away.

I quickly showered and headed to the call room, after getting my props in place. I turned on the television and watched Maury. I loved seeing how the ladies run in the back and fall on the floor, all because the paternity test came back negative. I think some of those ladies should be thankful the potential deadbeat fathers are not their baby daddy.

I had been watching the program for about fifteen minutes when I received the first call.

"Fantasy, how can Saucy help you, babe?"

"Um, my man and I want the threesome package." She giggled nervously.

"Do you want a man or a woman?"

"A man, honey," she said proudly.

"No, hell, you don't!" A male voice yelled in the background.

"You told me I could choose what I wanted, and I want another man," she yelled back.

"I didn't know you were going to choose that!" He replied.

I snickered to myself as they continued.

"I don't see what the problem is. You chose the last time, and we had a woman. Now I want a man!"

"That shit ain't gone happen! You can hang up the phone, a matter of fact. I don't even want it no more!"

"What are you doing?"

"Putting on my damn clothes!"

"Why!"

"I told you I'm done!"

The line went dead, and I hung up the phone. I had a good laugh. They really made my day.

Three o'clock came and went with no sign of Ty. I called him several times, and each call went to his voice mail. I knocked on David's room door.

"Yeah," he answered. This usually meant to come in, so I opened the door.

"David, are you busy?"

"Nope, just surfing the ethernet."

"Will you drop me off at the hair salon? Ty has my car."

"Sure, let me get my keys."

"Thanks."

As always, it was busy when I stepped into Belinda's salon. She has two other stylists, Kevin and Joy, to help her with the overflow of customers. However, Joy had been my stylist since I moved out to L.A. I wasn't seated in the chair five minutes before Belinda started with her questions.

"So, what you been up to chick?" She asked.

"Not a thing," I yawned. "Just work and home."

"I hear you. You must have had a long night. I see you yawning and all." She winked.

"Nope, as a matter of fact, I had an early morning. I started my day with a run before working my shift."

"Get it, girl. I wish I was that disciplined." She turned her attention back to her client.

Belinda isn't fat, but on her five-foot frame, she could stand to lose about twenty pounds, and maybe tone it up a little bit. Anyway, I tried to keep my conversation short with her because I knew she loved to gossip, and I didn't need her twisting anything I said.

I had been in the salon two hours before Ty called me back.

"Where the hell are you in my car?" I snapped, not really caring if the other customers heard me or not.

"Girl quit tripping. I'm on my way."

"You better be," I retorted. Ty was working my last nerve, and I was very close to letting him have it.

"Is everything alright?" Joy asked.

"It will be," I said, putting my earbuds in my ear and hitting the playlist button on my phone. The first song was Don't Mean It by Tyler Dumont. I love that song, especially the second verse, when she says, 'I'm doing me now.' That's where I'm at mentally. I don't want to be with Ty or anyone else. I'm done with relationships.

Autumn

I looked over at the small clock that sat on my nightstand. It was 8:45 am. I had awakened with Destini on my mind. I wanted to give her a call, but we grew up with a house rule; 'no calls before ten in the morning and no later than ten at night.'

My thoughts quickly shifted to Antwan. I laid there a few minutes, trying to decide if I should call the LA Times to see if he worked there. I didn't want to come off thirsty, which is why I was going to talk to Destini, before making the decision to pursue him.

Although I'm twenty-one and full of wisdom, thanks to Aunt Mattie, I'm not that experienced when it comes to men. I've had my share of dates, but once they found out I wouldn't put out, they would leave, which is fine by me because it just proved they only wanted one thing, and I made a vow to myself that I would refrain from sex until I'm married. I know the right one would come along and appreciate who I am and respect my decision to wait.

Just make the call Autumn. What do you have to lose? I googled LA Times and dialed the number. The receptionist answered the phone on the first ring.

"LA Times, Marsha speaking, how may I help you?" She asked.

"Do you have an Antwan working there?" I replied.

"What's his last name?"

Like a ton of bricks, it hit me. I didn't even know his last name. How was I going to search for someone I don't even know?

"Never mind," I said, ending the call. I felt so stupid. Here I was trying to find someone who was obviously not interested in me.

After taking a quick shower and getting dressed, I headed to Melissa's Java Cafe to meet Zora for lunch. When I turned into the parking lot, I spotted her car right away. I parked and walked into the cafe. Zora was sitting in a booth in front of the large tinted window.

"Hey," I said, taking a seat across from her.

"Hey." She smiled.

"Melissa has done a great job with this place," I said, noticing the new décor. The walls were painted sage green with cream trim, and the floor was a light gray with creamed faux wood tile. The furnishings were dark brown. Each booth had dark green padding framed by dark brown wood, and there was a blend of fall colors in the paintings displayed on the wall.

"Yes, she has," Zora agreed. "So, girl, you know I'm dying to know what Anna had to say about that situation with Ty."

I shook my head. "She pretty much said nothing. At least nothing that I believed anyway."

"Well, what did she say?" Zora leaned forward, anxiously waiting for my response.

"She blames herself for the beating because she let a guy buy her a drink while Ty was in the restroom."

"What kind of shit is that!"

"That's what I said to her. I told you she didn't say much of anything."

"Yeah, she did. She told you a lie. I don't believe that."

I nodded my head in agreement. "Girl, let me tell you about this guy I met on the plane," I said, changing the subject.

"Hold up, you met someone on the plane and didn't tell me about it yesterday when I picked you up from the airport? Shame on you!" She said crossing her arms.

I dismissed her comment with a wave of my hand and continued talking. "Anyway, his name is Antwan."

"Antwan, who?"

"I don't know. I didn't ask him what his last name was." I sighed.

She shook her head in disbelief. "Autumn, how did you not get his name? You sat next to him on the plane for four hours."

I shrugged my shoulders. "I wasn't thinking. I guess I figured I would get the chance to ask him later since we had talked about getting together for dinner, while we were in Chicago."

"Well, does he live in LA?"

"Yes, I think so. He said he works for the LA Times."

"LA Times? What does he look like?"

"He's about average height for a man, light complexion, but looks like he could be bi-racial, and it's obvious he lifts weights because he has muscular build- What are you doing?" I asked as she looked through her phone.

"I'm asking Google. Google knows everything," she said with a wink and a smile.

I sighed. "Yeah, that's what they say."

She held her phone in front of my face, so I could view the screen. "Is this him?"

"Yes," I responded with a massive grin on my face. There was his photo, and beside it was his name with a small caption. Twenty-one-year-old, Antwan Jacobs, joins LA Times as an investigative journalist.

"Call him," Zora urged.

"You think I should?"

"Yes, I think you should."

I took my phone out of my purse and dialed the number. I was both nervous and excited at the same time. I felt as though butterflies were performing a dance routine in my stomach.

"Hello, LA Times, Jacquelyn speaking, how may I help you?"

"May I speak with Antwan Jacobs, please?"

"He is out of the office today. Would you like to leave a message on his voicemail?"

"No, thanks. I will try back later. Can you tell me when he will be back in his office?"

"He is out of town on assignment. He should be back next week."

"Okay, thank you," I said before hanging up the phone. "Well, so much for that." I placed my phone back in my purse. "He is out of town on an assignment until next week," I said, disappointedly.

"I think you should have left your number." She shrugged.

"And why is that?"

"Because he has to check in at some time or another, and they could give him your information."

"No, ma'am. I am not going to do that. I will try again next week. If I get him, fine. If I don't, then I'm letting it go and moving on," I said in a matter-of-fact tone.

Zora didn't reply, but she shook her head in disagreement and picked up the menu. "I'm hungry, what are you going to have?" She asked, scanning over the food choices.

"I'm getting the usual. A chicken salad sandwich with fries and tea."

"I think I'll have the same." She put the menu down and waved for the waitress.

"I'm moving out of the house," Zora announced after we placed our orders.

"Why?" I was caught off guard by the news, and I knew she could see it on my face. I didn't want her to go. She was all I had in LA, and I depended on her a lot.

"I'm moving in with Omar."

"But Zora, you haven't been dating him that long; don't you think your moving too fast?"

"No, I don't, and I've made my decision."

I sat back in the booth and pouted. "I don't want you to go."

She smiled, "You will be okay. I will still be here for you."

I knew things were going to change once she moved in with her boyfriend, and there was nothing I could say to change her mind. She was in love, and that was all that mattered in her world. I smiled, "I'm happy for you, Zora."

"Thank you." She winked.

Chloe

"This is gorgeous!" I exclaimed as I looked at myself in the mirror. "Marie, it's beautiful." Tears fell as I became overwhelmed with joy. Marie handed me a tissue and gave me a hug as I wiped away the tears.

"I'm glad you love it." She smiled.

Marie had designed, and custom made my wedding dress. It was a one-shoulder strap with a sweetheart neckline. It was made with a cream chiffon fabric that contoured the curves of my body perfectly, and the beading on the dress gave it a more sophisticated look.

"I really do." I smiled, wiping away more tears. "You have outdone yourself." I twirled around and admired myself one more time before stepping off the platform to change. "Marie, is it okay if I leave my dress here? I don't want Devin to see it until the day of the wedding."

"Sure, no problem. I'll keep it safe. I have a room here just for that sort of thing."

She placed the dress back into the white garment bag and wrote my name on a pink slip, then she stapled it to the top of the bag and walked towards the back of the store with me following behind her. When she opened the door to the room she was speaking of, there were two racks full of wedding gowns.

"Are all of these dresses of women that are getting married?" I asked, amazed at how many were in the room.

"Yep. They are all waiting on their special day."

"Wow," is all I could say. It had to be at least thirty dresses between the two racks. Marie added my dress to the collection, and we made our way back to the front of the store.

When I got in my car, I called Sherri, our wedding planner. Devin and I are getting married in Miami in less than five months, so I try to contact Sherri at least twice a month to stay informed on what she's doing on her end.

"Hello, Exquisite Events Miami," Maci answered.

"Hi, Maci, is Sherri in?"

"Yes, she is, but she's with a client at this moment."

"Will you have her to give me a call when she's done?"

"Yes, I will?"

"Okay, thanks."

I pushed the disconnect button on the steering wheel and turned up the radio. Talk by Khalid was playing.

I sang along while cruising down the street. Nah, it can't be, I said, catching a glimpse of a guy walking down the sidewalk. He looked like someone from my past, and if it was who I thought it was, then it could only mean one thing-trouble. I made a U-turn at the intersection. By the time I made my way back to where I had seen him, he was gone. Maybe it wasn't him, I thought while taking a deep breath to calm my nerves.

Belinda

"Anna, if you need me to take you home, I really don't mind. Ty isn't coming," I said, getting ready to leave for the day. We were closed, and everyone had left except me because I was waiting for Anna's ride to arrive.

"No, thanks. My ride is on the way."

I rolled my eyes and sat down to play a game on my phone. When the door opened, I looked up, and my girlie spot began to tingle at the sight of the chocolate statue that stood before us.

"You ready?" he asked Anna.

She nodded, and he turned to leave. "See you later, Belinda," she said as she was getting ready to walk out the door behind him.

"Hey, aren't you going to introduce me to your friend?"

"Nope."

I walked out behind her. "Hey, don't you know it's rude not to speak when you walk into a building?" He turned around and smiled, which caused my heart to skip.

"I'm sorry. Hello, how are you?" he replied.

"Now that's more like it, I'm doing fine." I smiled and held out my hand. "My name is Belinda, what's yours?" I asked.

"Really, Belinda." Anna interrupted.; She stood on the passenger side of the car with her hand on her hip.

I ignored her. "Your name, honey?"

"It's David."

"Nice to meet you, David," I said, shaking his hand. "Your girlfriend here is very rude. I hope you are nothing like her." I pointed to Anna.

"Oh, she's not my girlfriend. We're co-workers."

"Get in the car, David. She already knows who I'm dating." Anna opened the car door and sat down.

"Go ahead and take her home before she makes me catch a case." I retorted.

He laughed.

"Don't be a stranger. You're welcome anytime."

Call me, I mouthed, pretending I had a phone. He chuckled and nodded his head before getting in the car. I turned and sashayed back into the salon, making sure he got a good look at my apple bottom. I may be about five years his senior, but he can take a dive in my pool any time he wants.

Anna

"Can you believe her?" It was more of a statement than a question. I shook my head. "She was feeling you."

"Nah, she was just playing." David adjusted his position in his seat.

"Yeah, right, she was serious."

He smiled. "You think so? Do she have a man?"

"Yep, she's married," I said, amazed that he was even inquiring.

He shook his head. "Looks like ole boy better get on his job before a brother like me get his woman and blow her back out."

"You wouldn't." I turned in the seat to look at him.

He looked at me and shrugged his shoulders. "What? I don't discriminate. I love the thick ones, too."

I slapped him on his shoulder playfully. "You're too much."

There was silence between us for about a minute before he spoke again.

"I'm going to have Geno go with you and Ty to meet the connect."

Surprised, I asked, "Since when have we started letting the workers meet with the connect?"

"Since I promoted him. Geno has been working for me for a long time. I trust him, he's loyal, and he gets the job done."

I couldn't argue with that. Everything he said about Geno was true. I would rather work with him than Ty any day. "Okay, you're the boss. So, when is our next meeting?"

"Next Saturday. The usual spot."

"Alright, I'll let Ty know."

"Yeah, one more thing. Whatever you two got going on, squash it."

I nodded. I wanted Ty out of my life. He had been nothing but a great disappointment to me since we got in the game. After the money started flowing in, he started being stupid like buying two seventy's model Chevy Monte Carlo's. He spent a lot of money getting them refurbished, then had the nerve to have one painted lime green with twenty-eight-inch rims and the other a bright orange with thirty-two-inch rims. David made him take them both to the chop shop. Personally, I wouldn't have bothered to buy a second vehicle and make it flashy after having to get rid of the first one, but Ty, he stupid like that.

It wasn't until late that night when Ty returned my car. He didn't even have the decency to call me and let me know he had brought it back. After calling him several times and not getting a response, I contemplated calling the police but changed my mind. I didn't need his dumbass in jail. We had work to do, and the last thing I needed was to make David angry, especially after he had just warned me to squash things with Ty.

When I awakened the following morning, I called him, and to my surprise, he answered on the first ring.

"Yeah."

"Bring me my damn car now, or I'm calling the police?" I threatened.

"You need to calm the hell down. Your car is in your driveway."

"Where are my keys?"

"They are in the car."

I pushed the end call button and hurried downstairs, just before I opened the door, David stopped me.

"Are these what you're looking for?" He asked, dangling the keys in the air.

"Yes, how did you get them? Ty said he left them in the car."

"He did. I heard him when he pulled up last night. I saw him get out of your car into another one, so I went outside to check it out."

"Thank you," I said, taking the keys out of his hand. So, how does it look?" I asked, walking towards the door.

"It's fine, there's no damage." He sat down in the wing back chair and took a sip from his cup.

"Well, that is good to hear," I responded as I exited the house. David was right, the car was fine, but my mood wasn't. I know one thing; he will not be getting my car again. His ass can walk for all I care.

Autumn

"So, what are you getting today?" Belinda asked, bringing me out of my musing.

"I want highlights and an updo. I'm going to a red-carpet event, so I need a classy look for tonight?" I said, smiling from ear to ear.

Antwan was working an event hosted by Essence, and I was his plus one.

It had been two weeks after my lunch with Zora before I got a chance to speak with Antwan. Since then, we talked every day for the past month. We went on a couple of dates, and they were wonderful. He makes me laugh, smile, and I still get those butterflies each time I hear his voice. We had a connection that I just couldn't describe. It's like we are soulmates. I'm glad I listened to Zora and called him again. I tried to contact him the week after our lunch, and he was not there. I decided to move on, but Zora kept pushing, so I tried again, and a few days later, I got him.

"Well, he must be something else, honey. Got you glowing and acting like you in love and everything."

"Mhmm." Joy responded. "I'm not mad at you girl, do your thing." She chuckled.

"I know that's right, honey, ain't nothing like young love," Kevin chimed in.

"Okay, so, what are you wearing?" Belinda asked.

"I have a picture of my dress right here," I took my cellphone out of my pants pocket, and pulled the picture up to show her.

"Ahhhh, sookie sookie, now!" Belinda said while doing a two-step dance move across the floor. "This dress is on fire!"

"Let me see," Joy said.

"Me too," Kevin replied, as they both stood beside Belinda to get a better view of the dress.

"Belinda, you got to work your magic on her head, honey. She got to stop traffic when she walks out in that dress, babe," Kevin said with a snap of his fingers.

"I know that's right." Joy agreed.

They both walked back to their stations, and Belinda began to work on my hair. When she finished, I felt like a princess. My hair was pinned in a curly bun decorated with a little hair jewelry and a couple of wavy curls hanging down to frame each side of my face. The style complimented my face beautifully. Belinda had done her magic indeed, and I was one happy customer.

Belinda

"What do you two have planned for tonight?" I asked Joy and Kevin as we closed the salon.

"Well, I plan to go home, shower, pour me up a glass of wine, and watch Hallmark movies all night," Joy replied.

"Girl, please! On a Saturday night," Kevin retorted, shaking his head in disagreement. He waved Joy off. "Well, honey, Mitch and I are meeting up at Club Xtreme at nine for drinks." Kevin gyrated his hips "and a little nightcap afterward if you know what I mean."

"Ooh, you such a hoe," Joy responded.

"Call me what you want, but at least I get mine," Kevin started twerking. He dropped it low and came back up before giving his derriere one last shake. "You need to get you some. Then maybe you won't be so uptight."

"Oh, I get mine in, believe that."

"Sure, you do, Joy, sure you do." Kevin turned to me and rolled his eyes. "Honey, the only dick she's getting is one that requires batteries. That's why she has that fucked up attitude."

"Fuck you, Kevin."

"See," he said as if her response proved his point.

Joy gave him the one-finger-salute and turned her attention back to me.

"So, what are you doing tonight?" She asked.

"I don't know. Ricky is working, so I may go catch a movie."

Kevin rolled his eyes. "You two are some sad heifers. Why not just join Mitch and me at the club for drinks?"

"I don't know. I'm really not feeling like clubbing tonight," Joy rebutted.

"I'll come. I can use a night out." I said, putting up the last of my hair products.

"Come on, Joy, it will be fun," Kevin said, trying to persuade her.

"Yeah, let's do it," I chimed in.

Joy looked from me to Kevin. "Okay, count me in." She smiled. "I'll meet you all there."

Club Xtreme was on fire that night. The building was packed, the energy was high, and the dance floor was full. I was having the time of my life, dancing, and enjoying friends.

"Kevin, order me another cosmopolitan," I said as I got up to join the others in a line dance on the floor.

After two more songs, the DJ played a slow jam. I was walking back to the table when someone grabbed my hand. I turned around, and to my surprise, it was David, Anna's friend. He looked just as delicious as I remembered from our last encounter.

"May I have this dance?" He asked.

I nodded and took his hand as he led me through the crowd. He pulled me into his arms, and instantly the nerves in my body awakened. The smell of his cologne was hypnotic, and I was under his spell. Our hips moved as one to the rhythm of the beat.

"You look beautiful tonight," he whispered in my ear.

I raised my head to say thank you, and he brushed his lips against mine. He immediately studied my face to see my reaction. I placed my hand on the side of his cheek and lifted my mouth to his. I let out a soft moan when our tongues touched and intertwined. As we swayed with the music, I could feel the growing bulge of his arousal through the fabric of his clothing. My pearl began to throb, causing an aching need deep within my center. I closed my eyes and imagined the two of us dancing in the nude. Our bodies, moving to one rhythm, and our hearts to one beat. My thoughts were interrupted when the DJ changed the flow of music from slow to upbeat.

"Oh, no, you don't," David said, pulling me back to him as I attempted to walk off the dance floor. "I can't leave right now." He pointed to his erection, and the crook of my mouth curled into a smile. He licked his lips seductively. "I see you're getting a kick out of this, huh."

"Maybe, just a little." I teased, drawing my bottom lip between my teeth.

We danced to the following two songs; both were fast pace. I was thankful for that because I don't think I could have handled another slow jam.

After dancing, we went back to the table where Kevin and Mitch were sitting people watching.

"This is David, Anna's friend. David, this is Kevin and Mitch," I said, introducing them.

"Hey," Kevin said, nodding his head.

Mitch held out his hand to give David a handshake. "Hey, man."

David shook his hand and sat down next to me at the table.

"Where is Joy?" I asked.

"I don't know, but you heifers, better get your drinks. We didn't come here to table watch all night," Kevin stood and polished off the last of his drink. "Now, we are going to dance."

Mitch stood and followed behind him. "Thanks, guys," I yelled as they disappeared into the crowd.

Autumn

"Oh, my God, Antwan! I've had the time of my life!" I said as we exited the building. "Tonight was amazing. I got to see so many celebrities and, and-,"

"And what?" He looked puzzled.

"And I don't know how I could ever repay you, but thank you so much for this experience."

"You owe me nothing. If anything, I feel privileged to have such a beautiful woman on my arm."

I smiled. "Well, in that case, you're welcome." We both laughed.

"I see you have jokes."

"Just a little." I made the gesture with my thumb and index finger.

The valet attendant drove up with his car and handed him the keys. We got in and fastened our seatbelts.

"Where to now?" I asked, adjusting myself in the seat.

"How does Charley's sound?"

"Sounds good to me."

Charley's was more of an upscale meet and greet bar. I had been there once with Zora and Omar on a blind date that she had set me up on, which turned out to be a disaster. From then on, it was no more blind dates for me.

"Looks like Charley's is busy tonight," I said, taking notice of the number of cars in the parking lot.

"Yep, looks that way," he said, trying to find a parking space.

After being seated and placing our drink orders, I asked Antwan about the Byron Jefferson story.

"So, any updates on that CEO of Princeton Enterprises?"

"As a matter of fact, there is," he said as he leaned in. "So, you know I interviewed that inmate, Richard Madison, right?" I nodded my head, and he continued. "Well, how about he's telling me he has a baby boy from his ex who's dating the husband of the woman who was charged in the attempted murder of Byron. How crazy is that?"

You just don't know. After I took a sip of my drink, I said, "Sounds to me like Richard is trying to get rumors started, and he's using the media to do it."

"Yeah, I thought about that, but what's his angle?"

I shrugged my shoulders. "Who knows? Maybe he wants to cause problems for his ex. Have you talked to her yet?"

"No, I really hadn't considered doing any additional reports on this story, but he has been relentless about getting this information out there."

"It's about mon-" I paused. "Oh, hell, no!"

"What?" Antwan turned to see what I was fixated on. "Do you know them?"

"Yeah, he's my roommate's boyfriend, and that's not my roommate," I said in a low annoyed tone. "I'm going over there."

"And do what? This is not the place for that," he said, looking around the room at the other customers.

"You're right, but I don't care." I got up from the table and sashayed my ass right over to Ty's table.

"Hey, Ty." I smiled. He looked like a deer caught in headlights "How have you been? I leaned in to hug him. I turned to his date. "Hi, I'm Autumn, and you are?"

"Felicia," she said, looking back and forth between Ty and me. I held out my hand.

"Nice to meet you, Felicia." We exchanged a handshake. "You two have a good night." I turned and walked back to our table, where Antwan had been watching my every move. When I sat down, he let out a light chuckle.

"What?" I asked.

He shook his head. "You are something else."

"I'll drink to that." I raised my glass before taking a sip of the drink.

Dinner was great, but I couldn't seem to stay focused. All I wanted to do was get home, and tell Anna about that no-good piece of shit she calls a boyfriend.

Belinda

I stirred under the covers just before my cell phone vibrated. I opened my eyes. Where the hell am I, and why is my head pounding? I looked over and saw David lying next to me asleep. "Oh shit!" My cell phone vibrated again, this time I picked it up and looked at the caller id.

"Hello," I answered.

"Belinda, where the hell are you?" "Ricky has been blowing my phone up, looking for you? Kevin snapped.

"What did you tell him?"

"I told him you left with Joy."

"Okay, good."

"Not good. He called Joy, and she told him you left with me."

"Damn."

"Girl, where your ass at?"

"Look, I'll talk to you later, okay," I pushed the end call button disconnecting the call. I scanned my phone, which displayed five missed calls from Ricky, four missed calls from Kevin, three missed calls from Joy, and two missed calls from Chloe. I jumped out of bed, and David sat up.

"Good morning, beautiful."

"Not now, David." I put on my pants. "Where is my bra?"

"It's on the back of that chair." He pointed to the black chair at his desk. I turned to get it when I stopped right in my tracks. I was taken aback by the image I saw in the mirror. My hair was all over the place. My eyeliner was ruined, and what was shocking was the white substance under my nostrils.

"What the hell is this?" I asked frantically.

"What are you talking about?"

"This!" I pointed at my nose.

"What you think it is?"

"David, please tell me this is not powder. I don't do drugs!"

"Well, that's exactly what it is," he said matter-of-factly.

"How could you do this to me?"

"I didn't do anything to you. You wanted to party with me, so that's what we did."

I sat at the end of the bed and started crying. He sat next to me and placed his arm around my shoulders.

"Get the fuck away from me!" I said, snatching away from him. I finished getting dressed and walked towards the door.

"Belinda, how are you going to get home?"

"I'll call an Uber," I said before storming out of the bedroom. Anna was standing in her doorway.

"I'll give you a ride home," she offered. After she retrieved her keys and purse from her bedroom, we headed out the door. Just as Anna put the car in reverse, David came rushing out of the house. He came to my window, and Anna pushed the power button to let it down. He handed me a small silver pouch.

"Here, you're going to need this later," he said and backed away from the car.

"Fuck you, David!" I threw the pouch at him, and he bent down to picked it up. He threw it back in the window, this time making sure it landed in Anna's lap.

"Make sure she gets it."

Anna nodded and backed out of the driveway.

I cried all the way home, and Anna didn't say one word the entire way. When she pulled up to my house, she turned off the engine and faced me.

"No judgment," she said before continuing. "My advice to you is to throw this away and get treatment asap." She handed me the silver pouch of coke, and I put it in my purse.

I opened the door but closed it back. I looked at her, but couldn't form the words to speak.

"Don't worry. I'm not going to say anything," she assured me.

"Thank you," I replied, before getting out of the car.

Anna

When I returned home from dropping Belinda off, I went upstairs and knocked on David's bedroom door.

"Yeah," he called out.

"I want to talk to you," I entered his room and closed the door behind me.

"I figured you would, but it's none of your business."

"No, but come on, David. Belinda? She's a business-woman, not a party girl."

"Maybe you don't know her as well as you think you do," he said matter-of-factly. "I don't know what you think, you know, but I didn't force Belinda to do coke. She did it on her own."

"Yeah, but you could have stopped her."

"And just how was I supposed to do that? We were both intoxicated, and you know, when I'm drinking, I always have a little something extra to heighten my high. She saw me do it, and she wanted to try it. I told her no, but she grabbed it out of my hand and took a hit." He shrugged.

"Can I come in?" Autumn asked, knocking on the door.

"Yeah," David answered.

"Hey, Anna, can I see you for a minute?" she asked, standing in the doorway.

"Sure," I walked out of David's bedroom into my own, and Autumn followed behind me.

"What's up?" I asked as she closed the door.

"I saw Ty last night at Charley's." she paused, "with another woman."

"Oh," I said casually. "Well, I hope he makes her happy." I sat down on the bed.

"Okay, I'm confused. I thought you and Ty were a couple," she said, looking puzzled.

"We are, but I haven't been feeling him for a while now, so I'm actually happy to hear this information because I can get rid of him."

She chuckled. "Anna, you never cease to amaze me." We both laughed.

"So, what did she look like?" I asked.

She waved her hand. "Don't worry, honey, she can't hold a candle to you." She winked and exited the bedroom.

Chloe

I was standing face to face with my worst nightmare. My past had come back to haunt me. Derek Mason, aka "Smoke." One whom I considered a childhood friend until he expressed that he wanted more, but I wasn't about that thug life and wanted no parts of it.

"Aren't you happy to see me?" He asked, breaking my train of thought.

"What are you doing here?"

"I came to see you," he smiled, showing a top row of gold teeth.

"How did you know where to find me?"

"A little birdy told me." He opened his arms wide. "Can a brother get some love?"

"You can't be here," I said, stepping outside of the door and closing it behind me.

"Ah, come on now, don't be like that." He touched my hair, and I stepped away from him.

"You have to go now!" I tried to push him towards his car, but he wouldn't budge.

"After all, I've done for you, Peaches, you owe me."

"Listen, I need you to leave. I will call you, and we can talk later, but I am begging you to please go," I urged him.

He handed me a piece of paper out of his jacket. "Here's my number. Make sure I get that phone call, or I'll be back."

He got in his car and drove off. When I turned around, Devin was standing at the door.

"Who was that?" He asked.

"Just someone who needed directions."

"Hmm, it looked like more than someone wanting directions."

"That was all it was," I said, walking into the bathroom and locking the door.

I turned on the shower and cried. I thought about his words, 'You owe me,' and my body trembled. The truth is I would never be able to repay him. He did eight years in prison for me, and now he was back to collect.

Belinda

I unscrewed the vent from the wall in the laundry room and pulled out the vial of powder from its hiding place.

I opened the small bottle and poured the last of its content on the dryer. When I inhaled the white substance, a burst of energy came over me, and I felt like I could do anything. I heard Ricky walking down the hall and quickly cleaned up the residue, making sure to throw the empty bottle in the bottom of the trash can. I then went to the bathroom to clean my face. When I opened the door, Ricky was standing there.

"I'm heading to Home Depot to get another blade for the lawnmower."

"Okay. I'm going to the salon for a little while."

"The salon, on a Sunday?" He questioned.

"Yes, I need to get things ready for tomorrow."

He nodded and gave me a light kiss on the lips before leaving. I grabbed my purse and keys and headed out behind him. When I got in the car, I called David.

"Speak," he answered on the first ring. I cleared my throat.

"Um, this is Belinda. I need to see you.

"Why do you need to see me?"

"David, you know what I need, don't act like you don't."

"Alright, bet," he said, hanging up the phone.

I called him right back.

"What!" He answered, this time he sounded a little annoyed.

"Are you coming or not?"

"Yeah, where you at?"

"I'm at the salon."

"Okay." He hung up the phone again. I didn't realize he was such a dick, until that moment. I busied myself around the salon, mopping the floor, and straightening up the inventory. David arrived two hours later with the product, and I was feigning bad. When he entered the salon, he took the vial out of his pants pocket. When I tried to take it out of his hand, he held his arm up over his head so I couldn't get it.

"Hold up, shorty," he said, using his other arm to keep me at bay. "This is going to cost you."

"Cost me! This shit should be free. You, the one got me on it."

"Girl, you're tripping. I didn't do shit to you. You did it to yourself."

"Bullshit, and you know it!" I screamed.

"Hey, I didn't come here to argue with you. If you want it, it's gonna cost you sixty dollars."

I snatched my purse off the counter and counted out the cash in my wallet.

"I only have forty-five dollars on me. Can I pay you the rest later?"

"Hell, nah, that's not the way this works." He put the vial back in his pocket.

"Wait, I'll run to the bank and get the rest of it."

"Call me when you get it, I'm out." He turned to walk away, and I grabbed his arm.

"Please, I'll do anything." I pleaded.

He raised his eyebrows. "Anything?"

"Yes."

He unzipped his pants. "Then drop to your knees."

Anna

I went by Geno's to drop off his supply. We did our usual routine. I counted the money from the last transaction, and he inventoried the product.

"So, when is this big job?" He asked as he put away the bag of coke.

I shrugged my shoulders. "I don't know. David said he would let me know when it's time."

He nodded. "Cool. Let me ask you something, are you and Ty still kicking it?"

"Not really, but David wants us to work together until this job is done. So, I have to deal with him until then." I sighed heavily.

"Hmmm, I feel you."

"Why'd you ask?"

"Because I've seen his little punk ass out here. I was told he's seeing some chick in the building behind me."

"Oh," I said nonchalantly. "It's cool. I don't want him anymore. If it weren't for David, I would've been done with him." I walked to the door. "See you next week."

"Bet."

As I was leaving the complex, Ty was turning in. He stopped and rolled down the window. I looked at him and drove away. He turned around and followed me, blowing the horn and flashing the headlights, like a maniac on the street. When I didn't stop, he called me, but I didn't answer. Finally, he got the message and turned around.

When I got home, I looked at my phone, and just as I expected, I had messages in my voicemail. I entered the code and began listening to the recordings.

1st message: Hey, pullover.

2nd message: Oh, so you mad.

3rd message: I'm not going to chase your ass.

I tossed the phone on the bed. "Boy Bye," I said, feeling annoyed.

It was almost time for my shift at Fantasy, so I took the red phone out of my closet and plugged it into the wall. Then, I called Gina.

"Hello," she answered.

"Hey, I'm going to take calls in my room tonight. Just transfer the lines when you're shift is up and give me a call to let me know when you've done it."

"Okay, I will."

Shortly after I hung up with her, the red phone rang. I looked at my watch. I still had fifteen minutes before my shift started. Maybe it's one of my regulars, I thought, as I answered the phone.

"This is Spicy. What's your pleasure, babe?" I purred in the phone.

"Why you didn't stop when I was trying to holla at you?" Ty questioned, with a hint of anger in his voice.

"Why the hell are you calling the business phone?" I was annoyed.

"Because you won't answer your damn cell phone," he yelled.

"What do you want?"

"I want to talk to you."

"We have nothing to talk about. I know all about your bitch," I snapped.

"Look here, she's no bitch."

"Oh, so you're defending her now?"

"Nah, but you don't know her like that to be calling her a bitch."

"I don't need to know her, and this conversation is over," I said, slamming the phone down.

My door flew open, and Ty was standing there. His eyes were glazed with anger. "This conversation isn't over until I say it's over," he growled.

"Get the hell out of here." I pointed.

"I'm not going nowhere."

I got up and started pushing him out of my room. He stumbled and caught himself.

"Get out!" I yelled, pushing him again. He pushed me back, and I stumbled across the floor. He put his hand around my throat and started choking me. I scratched him across his face, and he punched me twice. Blood trickled into my mouth from my now busted lip. He removed his hand from around my throat and stood up. I kicked him in his balls, and he bent over in pain.

"You bitch!" He spattered and lunged for me again, but I managed to roll out of his way, and he landed on the bed. I got up and ran over to the dresser to grab the gun out of my purse. But, before I could get it, he grabbed my arms, slamming me into the wall. He drew his hand back to hit me again, but he was stopped abruptly. David had come to my rescue. I didn't know when he got home, but I was happy to see him. He snatched Ty up by his shirt and gave him a hard punch to his face. Ty fell to the floor, and David stood over him.

"If you touch her again, you're a dead man," he said, gritting his teeth. "Now get the hell out of here."

Ty scurried himself off the floor and ran downstairs. Before he opened the door to leave, David yelled down at him. "Hey! I'll call you later. Make sure you answer your phone."

Ty nodded and left.

David turned his attention to me. "I'll go get you some ice."

While he was gone, I stood in the mirror and looked at my face; two black eyes, a busted lip, and a swollen cheekbone. I held my head down and began to cry. There was a soft knock at the door, but I didn't answer.

Gina entered my room and gasped at the sight of me. "Oh my God, Anna, what happened!"

"Ty is what happened," I said, flinching at the mere feel of her touch.

"Anna, I'm so sorry."

"You have nothing to be sorry about. This is not your fault."

"No, but I let him in. If I'd known he was going to do this, I wouldn't have opened the door."

"Well, you couldn't have known it, and neither did I."

"Are you going to file a report?"

"I got it from here, Gina." David interrupted.

"Uh, okay," she said, standing to leave. "I'll check on you later." She gave me a warm smile. She turned just before leaving. "Don't worry about the calls. I'll take your shift. You get some rest."

"Thank you, Gina," I said as she closed the door behind her.

David handed me the ice bag, and I applied it to my face.

"Anna, I'm sorry. I didn't know things were this bad." He sat on the bed next to me.

"I can't work with him, David. I just can't," I said through tears.

"Listen, Anna, I'm going to need you to. I have a lot riding on this deal."

"But I can't do it. Look at me," I said sobbing.

He lifted my chin. "Believe me, I'm going to handle Ty. You are my girl, and what he's done is unacceptable. But right now, I need you to be on board with this. I'm depending on you."

I nodded and laid down across the bed. He placed one of the pillows under my head.

"I brought you something for pain." He handed me two pills and the bottle of water that was on the nightstand.

"What are these?" I asked, looking at the small white pills.

"Ibuprofen."

"I'll take them later."

He placed them back on the nightstand and stood to leave. "Try to get some rest."

"I will."

He turned off the bedroom light. "Call me if you need anything," he said before closing the door behind him.

Once he was gone, I got the pills and looked them up on the pill identifier site. They were ibuprofen. I took them both and laid back down, drifting off to sleep, shortly after that.

Autumn

"Good morning," I said, to McKenzie, during our FaceTime.

"Good morning. Hold on, let me go get Mercedes." I could see him walking through the living room and up the stairs.

"So, how have you been?" I asked.

"I'm doing great, and you?

"I'm okay."

He lifted an eyebrow. "Just okay?"

"Yeah, just busy with work. What are your plans today?" I asked, putting the focus on him.

"We're going to do a little shopping for MJ."

"Aw, I wish I was there. I really miss you guys," I said with a hint of sadness.

"We miss you too, baby." He refocused the camera so I could see all three of them.

"Hey, Mercedes. How are you?"

"I'm fine, baby girl. How about yourself?"

"I'm okay. I miss you guys."

"We miss you, too."

"I can't believe how big MJ has gotten," I said in awe at his chubby little frame.

"I know, right. I think it's breast milk," McKenzie said. Mercedes nodded her head in agreement.

"Well, I was calling this morning to tell you I may be coming to Chicago next week."

"Well, you know you are welcome anytime," Mercedes said.

"Yes, we will be happy to see you." McKenzie chimed in.

"I will be happy to see you all, too."

I told them how Richard had reached out to Antwan again, and he was considering talking to him. I wanted to be there for the meeting so I could personally hear what he had to say. Mercedes was okay with me sitting in on the interview, but McKenzie was apprehensive about it.

However, he had relented by the end of our conversation.

After hanging up the phone, I called Antwan.

"Hey, are we still on for dinner tonight?" I asked.

"Yes, I will pick you up around seven."

"Okay, how should I dress?"

"Dress casual. Tonight, I'm cooking dinner for you."

"Well, alright, then," I said cheerfully.

We talked a little longer and ended our call.

Antwan arrived at precisely seven o'clock, and I was ready to go. One thing I've learned while dating him for the past few months is, he's always on time, but I guess you've got to be in his line of work.

"Hi," I said, getting into the car.

"Hey." He kissed me and backed out of the driveway. "I hope you're hungry because I have a nice dinner cooked for us."

"Yes, I am." I smiled and fastened my seatbelt. "So, what did you cook?

"Ah, it's a surprise."

"Okay, I like surprises," I winked.

On the way to his house, we talked and sometimes stopped to sing along with the music on the radio, making the thirty-minute ride seemed more like fifteen instead. I guess it's true; time does fly when you're having fun.

Antwan lived in a high-rise apartment on the eighth floor of Santa Monica apartments.

"Oh my god, Antwan, this is beautiful," I said, entering his apartment. I placed my purse on the couch and walked over to the open bay window. The view of the ocean was gorgeous.

"I get that same feeling every time I come home," he said as he stood next to me.

I turned to face him. "Wow, I can only imagine."

He smiled. "Come, let me show you the rest of the place."

He took my hand and gave me a tour of the apartment; each room was as beautiful as the next, with teal blues and orange decors accentuating them throughout the space. The bedrooms also had an excellent view of the ocean and a balcony. We ended the tour in the kitchen. He picked up both flutes of wine and handed me one.

"Let's make a toast."

"Okay, to what?"

"A beautiful evening?" He smiled.

Walking over to the table, he pulled the chair out for me, after I was seated, he uncovered the plate.

"For you, madame." He bowed.

I giggled. "Well, thank you, dear sir. This looks amazing."

"Why thank you," he responded, taking his seat at the other end of the table.

Antwan had prepared baked lobster tail with a garlic-butter dipping sauce, rice pilaf, and steamed broccoli.

I dipped the lobster into the butter sauce and took a bite. "Mmmm, this is delicious," I said, as I enjoyed the combination of the sweet, delicate meat with the savory taste of the buttery sauce.

"Glad you think so."

We finished our dinner and went for a walk on the beach.

"Ah, I love the beach," I said, putting my feet in the water.

"So, do I. It's something about the water that is so serene."

"Exactly! You know Antwan; you get me, most men I've dated don't."

"That's because they weren't men." He leaned in and kissed me softly on the lips.

"You're right about that?" I agreed.

Back at Antwan's, I retrieved my overnight bag out of the trunk of his car before entering the building. I wanted to shower to remove any traces of sand from the beach.

After we both showered, we enjoyed a glass of wine out on the balcony while we talked, and people watched.

"I'm going to follow up on that story in Chicago," he announced out of nowhere.

"When?"

"I will be flying out next week."

"Can I go with you? I would love to see McKenzie and Mercedes while we're there."

"Sure. Actually, I was going to ask you to come with me."

"Awesome."

"There's one more thing I wanted to talk to you about." He studied my face.

"What's that?" I took a sip of the wine.

"I want you to meet my mom."

"Do she live in Chicago too?"

"No, she lives here in LA."

"Oh." It occurred to me that we haven't talked much about our families. I knew he had an older brother, but that was about the extinct of it. "So, when do I meet her?"

"Well, she's having a dinner party for family and friends."

"Wait, you're from LA?" I interrupted.

"Yep, born and raised."

"Why didn't you tell me that?"

"Because you didn't ask." He smiled.

"Okay, I'll give you that. So, what else do I not know about you, Mr. Jacobs?"

"That I'm falling in love with you." Closing the space between us, he pulled me into his arms and kissed me passionately.

"I love you, too."

He picked me up and carried me to his bedroom, where he laid me on the bed. He laid beside me and kissed me again, causing my flower to tingle. He unfastened the four buttons on my shirt and exposed my bra. Freeing one of my breasts from its hiding place, he clamped his mouth around my erected nipple and began flickering it with his tongue. Heat rose in my core, causing dampness to form between my thighs. He slid his hand in my shorts, and I stopped him.

"I'm sorry," he said, removing his hand.

"You've done nothing wrong. I need to tell you something."

He had a puzzled look on his face.

"I've, um," I said nervously, trying to find the words to say.

His look changed from confusion to concern. "Autumn, what is it?"

I took a deep breath. "I'm a virgin."

He smiled. "Is that it?" He held me in his arms and kissed my forehead. "We don't have to do anything until you're ready, okay."

Looking into his eyes, I said, "I'm ready."

Chloe

I hadn't heard from or seen Derek in a couple of days, but I knew I needed to reach out to him soon, or he would keep his word and show up at my house again. So, I went to Wal-Mart and purchased a TracFone. When I got in my car, I retrieved the piece of paper with his number on it from under the floor mat and called him.

"Speak," he ordered.

"Derek?"

"Who wants to know?"

"This is Chloe."

"Ah, Peaches. What's up, girl?"

"This is not a social call," I snapped. "What do you want from me?"

"Oh, so it's like that? I mean, a brother can't get any talk? After all, I went through for you?"

"Derek, I know you looked out for me. I really appreciate it, but you don't have to keep throwing it in my face."

"Yeah, I do Peaches because you're giving me attitude. Unsolicited at that," he retorted.

I softened my tone. "You're right, Derek. I'm sorry."

"Now, that's more like it."

I rolled my eyes and let out a quiet sigh. "So, when did you get out?" I asked, pretending to be interested.

"I've been out a few months now. Of course, you would've known that if you'd answered my letters."

"What letters? I haven't received any letters from you."

"Come on, Peaches. Stop playing?"

"Derek, I'm not playing. I didn't get any letters. I went to visit you once, and my name wasn't on the list, so I never went back. I always assumed you didn't want to hear from me, and I've never received any letters."

"Well, I have a box full of them addressed from you. So, if you didn't send them, then who did?"

"That's a good question, I wish I had an answer for you, but all I can say is, it wasn't me. What address was on the letters?"

"Monroe St."

"Derek, we moved off Monroe Street shortly after you were sentenced. So, whoever moved in that house after us, must have sent those letters."

"Well, whether you did or not, they kept me going. So, when can I see you?"

"Never! Listen, Derek. I'm grateful for what you did for me, but I can't see you. I need you to understand that-"

He laughed. "You're funny." The tone of his voice changed from friendly to sinister. "Meet me at the Dream Hollywood Hotel in an hour. Don't be late." He hung up the phone.

Something about the way he laughed made me feel uneasy. I made a quick stop by the house to get my pistol before heading to the hotel.

I arrived there at precisely one hour. I called him as I drove into the parking lot.

"Hello," he answered.

"I'm here."

"I'm at the bar."

When I walked into the bar, the first thing I noticed was there was no one in there. This made me feel uncomfortable. Derek had chosen a table by the window on the far-right side of the room. His eyes scanned my body as I walked over to the table.

"So, what's up?" I asked, sitting across from him. He didn't respond. "Derek, I know you didn't have me come all this way, so you can sit and stare at me. What-do-you-want?"

He sat back in his chair and tapped his fingers on the table. "I need you to do something for me."

"What do you need me to do, and is it legal? Because I'm not doing anything illegal."

"You know, Peaches. Let me make one thing clear. You're not running shit here, and I'm getting tired of that funky ass attitude you have. You better check yourself."

I knew he wasn't playing, but I had to stand my ground. Through clenched teeth, I said, "Stop wasting my time."

His lips curled into a smile. "You still feisty, I see." He shook his head. "Okay, look. I need you to make a drop for me."

I looked at him sideways. "You need me to make a what?"

"You heard me."

"Oh, no-no-no-no-no," I said, shaking my head. "I can't do that. I don't do drugs, and I damn sure don't deal them!"

"Lower your voice, dammit." He leaned forward. "Oh, you're going to, or that cop-boyfriend of yours is going to find out the truth about his precious little Chloe," he snarled.

I felt like my back was against the wall. I didn't want Devin to know that part of my life, and I knew Derek would tell him if I didn't do what he wanted. I've never hated anyone as much as I hated Derek at that very moment.

"If I do this, will we be even?"

"Not even close." He chuckled.

I stood up to leave. "Then I'll think about it."

"I'll be in touch," he said as I walked away.

Belinda

"**D**amn, Belinda, you look like death rolled over," Kevin said when I walked into the salon.

Joy didn't say anything, but I could tell by the look on her face she was in agreement with Kevin.

I dismissed him with the wave of my hand. "I don't have time for your shit today," I said before walking to my office. I sat at the desk and pulled the small vial out of my purse. Just as I took a sniff of the substance, my door flew open.

"Oh, hell, no miss thang!" Kevin closed the door behind him. "Belinda, what the hell is this? You're doing coke now?"

"Shhh, lower your voice," I whispered.

"Oh no, we got to have an intervention." He walked over to the door and opened it.

"No, we don't."

He yelled for Joy to come to the office.

"What's going on?" She asked when she entered the room.

"Nothing," I blurted.

"Lies!" Kevin retorted. "Belinda is doing coke."

"What!" Joy exclaimed.

"Lower your voice," I said.

"Belinda, you got to get some help," Joy said with compassion.

"That's right, girl, before that habit gets out of hand," Kevin agreed.

"I'm okay, guys. I have everything under control. I don't even use it every day. I just had a rough night and didn't sleep well, so I needed a little pick me up this morning." I smiled, hoping I could persuade them, so they would drop the subject.

"Nuh-uh, honey. You can try to sell it, but I ain't buying it. You need help," Kevin said.

"Okay, listen. Let's get to work, and we can finish this conversation when we're done with our clients," I suggested.

"Yeah, that's best, because I have to wash that relaxer out of Ms. Donna's hair," Joy said, standing to leave. Kevin and I followed her back out front to handle our clientele.

All-day, they both kept their eyes on me. After the last client left, the three of us sat down and talked. We agreed that if they saw a significant change in my habit, then I would go to rehab with no resistance.

Autumn

Antwan and I went to visit McKenzie and Mercedes after his interview with Richard. I have to say that Richard is a real conman. He told so many lies, I couldn't count them, and he also said some questionable things, but I figured I'd get the answers once we got there.

After we arrived and got settled, I brought up the interview. "Antwan talked with Richard today."

"Yeah, how did it go?" McKenzie asked.

"He told a bunch of lies," I blurted.

Antwan looked at me but didn't say anything. Instead, he focused on answering McKenzie's question. "It went okay, but if you don't mind, I would like to ask the two of you a few questions to clear some things up."

"Fine with me. I have nothing to hide," McKenzie replied.

"Okay," Mercedes greed as she sat next to McKenzie on the couch.

"Richard said he and Sharon were both seeing Byron. Is that correct?"

"Yes, it is," Mercedes answered.

"He said that the two of you were engaged to get married, and the baby you had is his."

"He's telling a damn lie," McKenzie retorted.

Mercedes patted him lightly on his thigh. She stood. "I'll be back." She walked into the dining room and reached on top of the china cabinet. She returned with an envelope in her hand. "Here you go," she said, handing it to Antwan. "Read it out loud."

Antwan opened the envelope. "This says that McKenzie Taylor is 99.99 percent the father of McKenzie Taylor Jr."

"That's correct. MJ is McKenzie's son. I have never been pregnant by Richard Madison."

"When did you get a DNA test done?" McKenzie asked.

"The day you went to the doctor for your physical. I asked Dr. Shore to do it for me."

McKenzie looked puzzled. "I didn't agree, nor did I sign for a DNA test."

"You did, you just didn't know it, but we can talk about this later."

"No, we can talk about this now." McKenzie was not happy, and we could see it all over his face.

Mercedes took a deep breath and let out a heavy sigh. "Okay, but you're not going to like it," she warned.

"I don't like it now." McKenzie retorted.

Antwan and I sat quietly listening to Mercedes explained how Richard contacted her shortly after MJ was born. She showed text messages where he was demanding to see MJ and was threatening to petition the judge to have visitation rights. I really don't know how that would have worked with him being in prison, but he frightened Mercedes enough that she got a DNA test done. After hearing what she had to say, McKenzie was angry and had even threatened to go visit Richard in jail. In the middle of McKenzie's tantrum, Antwan asked the question I so wanted to know the answer to.

"How did Sharon really die? Richard says the two of you murdered her so that you can be together."

Silence fell in the room. McKenzie and Mercedes looked at each other, then, all eyes were on me.

"Hold up, wait a minute. Why are they looking at you?" Antwan asked.

I kept my eyes on the two of them, not wavering. I said, "Sharon was my mom."

"Your mom!" Antwan exclaimed in disbelief. "Why didn't you say something?"

I shrugged. "Will you answer the question, please?" I asked McKenzie and Mercedes.

"Sweetheart, we didn't murder your mom. She pulled the gun on us. After she shot Mercedes in the arm, I tried to take it from her, but she fought me, and the gun went off." McKenzie said.

"Autumn, that's the truth," Mercedes chimed in.

She stood again and went upstairs. When she returned, she handed me a folder. Inside was the police report, the hospital, and the autopsy report. We reviewed each document. Afterward, Mercedes and McKenzie shared some memories of Sharon. We laughed, and we cried. By the time we left them, I was emotionally exhausted.

Antwan did a follow-up story, but it was one that Richard Madison would never forget because he exposed him for what he truly was a liar.

Anna

Since the fight with Ty, I had been in the house, hiding the two black eyes he gave me. The swelling was gone, and the darkness had disappeared from around my eyes. I was ready to get out and live again. My first stop was the hair salon. I had to get something done with my head because it was just shameful the way I looked.

When I walked into the salon, Joy was shampooing a client.

"Hey, Anna. I'll be with you in a minute," she said, looking up to see who came through the door. I nodded and took a seat.

"Where is everybody?" I asked, noticing there was only the client she was shampooing there and me.

"Kevin is off today, and Belinda is out doing God knows what." She shrugged. "She canceled all her morning appointments but should be here by lunchtime."

"Oh, okay."

I sat quietly, flipping through the magazines until I heard the young lady say to Joy, 'Tyson is taking me to the Cardi B concert.'

My heart began to pound. I could almost feel it in my chest.

"Ah, I like Cardi B," I said, joining the conversation.

"Girl, she's the bomb," she replied.

"Yeah, you and Um, Tyson, right." She nodded. "You guys are going to have fun. They say she puts on an outstanding performance."

"That's what I heard," she agreed.

"I know a Tyson who's friends with my brother. Is his last name Marks, by any chance?"

"Yes, it is," she confirmed with a grin on her face. Joy looked at me and shook her head no. I ignored her and kept talking.

"Well, I'll have to tell Tyson I saw you." I smiled. "What's your name?"

"It's Felicia."

"Nice to meet you, Felicia."

"Nice to meet you, too. Tyson is picking me up, so you will have a chance to see him." She smiled.

"Good." I smiled back and continued looking at the magazine. I couldn't wait to see that bastard. I haven't heard from him since the fight, but I got something for that ass, though.

I waited until Joy was styling Felicia's hair before I left to go to the restroom. I retrieved the gun from my purse and placed it at the small of my back. I was thankful I had worn an oversized shirt because it covered it perfectly.

When Ty peeped his head in for Felicia, I jumped out of the chair and rushed him. I think he was startled because he didn't have much reaction time when I punched him in his face. Felicia and Joy came outside behind me. I tried to hit him again, but he grabbed my arm, pushing me away. Joy and Felicia stood between us.

"Bitch, I'mma kill your ass!" He sputtered, wiping the blood from his mouth.

I pulled the gun from behind me and pointed it at him.

"Yeah, try it." I dared him. "You will be one dead son-of-a-bitch today. Move out the way, Joy," I ordered.

She shook her head, no. "Anna, don't do this. He's not worth it, honey."

"Nah, Joy. This nigga whipped my ass a couple of weeks ago. Gave me two black eyes."

Felicia stood in shock. I looked at her.

"Yeah, this piece of shit right here beats women." I spat. "If he hasn't beaten your ass, it's just a matter of time before he does."

"Don't believe this bitch," he said, staring at me. "Felicia, get in the car." She didn't move. It was as if she was in a trance. "Get in the car, dammit!" He yelled at her.

She looked at him and went to the passenger side of the car.

"Please, Anna, put the gun away," Joy pleaded. I could hear sirens blaring in the distance.

"Consider this your lucky day. If you ever put your hands on me again, I will kill you," I warned.

He jumped in his car and sped off, with Felicia looking horrified.

Joy and I walked back inside. When the police arrived, all the on-lookers pointed the officers to the salon.

"Hey, we were told there was a disturbance here," one of the two officers said.

"No, no disturbance here. It's just my client and me," Joy responded.

"So, you're trying to tell us that all those people out there are lying?" The second officer replied.

Joy shrugged. "What you want me to tell you? There's no disturbance, officer. Everything is cool here. You see." She waved her arm around to get her point across.

"So, what you want to do?" The other officer asked.

"Well, with no victim, and no complainant, there's no crime." He looked at us. "You ladies have a good day," he said as they exited the salon.

A few minutes later, my cell phone rang.

"Hello," I answered.

"How long before she's done with your hair?" David asked.

"About an hour."

"Meet me at the house in two hours," he ordered, before hanging up. He was not happy, and I knew it had something to do with what just happened.

When I got to the house, David, Geno, and Ty were sitting in the den, each with a drink in his hand.

"Have a seat," David ordered.

"Well, can I get a drink first before joining this party?"

He gave me a look that said he meant business, and this was not the time to play. I passed up the drink and sat down.

"Obviously, you two are not taking me seriously when I say, knock off this bullshit you got going on."

"Dav-" Ty was cut off by David before he could finish saying his name.

"One more incident and both of you will be dead. You are not going to fuck up this deal for me. Do I make myself clear?"

Ty and I nodded our heads.

"Geno." David nodded.

Geno stood, grabbed Ty's hand, and broke two of his fingers. Ty screamed in agony from the pain.

David looked at me. "Am I clear?"

"Yes," I said, thankful he didn't punish me.

Geno reset Ty's fingers and wrapped them in a splint. While Geno finished up with Ty, David and I went to his bedroom. He handed me a pink and black gym bag.

"I need you to go to the subway station at Perishing Square. Go into the lady's restroom on the west side of the building. Someone will be waiting for you there."

I unzipped the bag. "How much is in here?" I asked.

"Ten grand."

I nodded and zipped the bag up as he proceeded to give me the instructions.

Perishing Square was busy. It was rush hour, and there were a lot of people coming in and out of the station, which is why David had picked this location. I parked my car and grabbed the bag out of the back seat. As I walked towards the restroom, I saw a lady going inside with the same bag. It was not until I entered the bathroom behind her that I was in for a shock, and so was she. I put my finger to my mouth to gesture her to be silent. After checking under each stall to make sure we were in there alone. I spoke.

"Chloe, what the hell are you doing here?"

Tears began to roll down her face.

"Stop it. Now is not the time. I need you to stay focused," I commanded.

She nodded her head and wiped the tears away. After we exchanged bags, I checked the product and told her to leave.

"I'll call you," I said before she walked out the door.

I waited twenty minutes before exiting the restroom. I made it back home with no incident. Once I handed over the bag to David, I went to my room and called Chloe. She confirmed that she had made it home, but couldn't talk because Devin was there, so we planned to meet the following day.

Chloe

"Hey, Anna," I said, stepping aside so she can enter the house.

"Hey, how are you?" she asked, taking a seat on the couch.

"Girl, what's up with you? I didn't know you were in the game."

"I'm not. I'm being blackmailed. But let's talk about you being in the game," I responded.

"Blackmailed by who?" She adjusted herself on the couch and didn't respond to my statement about her being in the game.

"By a former friend. It's a long story," I said, looking down at my hands, for no apparent reason.

"I have nothing but time."

It was obvious she wouldn't let me off the hook that easy. I studied her carefully. Although apprehensive, I had to talk to someone. I had to reveal this secret that has haunted me for a long time.

"Anna, you have to promise me, you won't say a word to anyone about what I'm getting ready to tell you."

"Scout's honor." She crossed her index and middle fingers.

"Okay." I inhaled. "When I was sixteen years old, I use to sneak out of the house at night to go hang out with my friends. Well, one night, I snuck out and went to a party. When I got ready to leave, my friend Derek walked me home like he usually did whenever we all got together. He would stand by the big oak tree across the street and wait for me to turn the light on in my bedroom, which let him know I had made it in safe. However, on this night, all of that changed. As I crossed the street to my house, Mr. Bobby, our neighbor, called me over to him before I opened the gate. I thought nothing of it because he and his wife, Mrs. Marilyn, are always asking us to do things for them. I did, however, find it odd that he would want something from me at two o'clock in the morning, but I went anyway. I waved Derek off, and he left. Or so I thought.

When I approached the porch, Mr. Bobby asked if I would read the letter he had in his hand because he couldn't read that well. I told him, yes, but I needed some light. He asked me to step inside. He didn't want to turn the porch light on because he didn't want to disturb the neighbors, so I followed him in the house. At first, everything seemed okay. Then out of nowhere, he grabbed me from behind and covered my mouth. He kicked the door shut and began forcing me towards the back of the house, as I tried to break away from his hold. Suddenly, he let out a painful cry and let me go. When I turned around, Derek was standing there, and boy was I happy to see him, but Mr. Bobby was angry. He punched Derek in the face, so I jumped on his back to stop him, but he flung me off him onto the floor. Derek got in a couple of punches before Mr. Bobby put him in a chokehold. That's when I grabbed a knife out of the drawer and stabbed him in the neck. He let Derek go and pulled the knife out before he collapsed to the floor. I didn't know until later that I had hit his main artery. Anyway, he died, and Derek took the rap for me. He did eight years in prison for voluntary manslaughter, and now he wants payment."

"So, making drops for him is your payment?"

"Yes. Anna, but I can't do this. I'm so afraid, and I don't know what to do." My eyes filled with tears.

"So, when is your next drop?"

"I don't know. Yesterday, was my first drop."

"Okay, well, that was to see if he could trust you."

"What do I do now?"

"Nothing. The next time Derek gives you a call, you let me know." She wrapped her arms around me. "I got you, Chloe. We are both getting out of this shit."

I inhaled a deep breath. For the first time, I felt relieved since Derek forced his way back into my life.

Belinda

"Listen, I'm sending someone over there to drop it off," David's said with agitation in his voice. Perhaps, he was pissed at the way I'd been blowing his phone up. I had called him five times before he called me back.

"Yeah, I got you," I said, hanging up the phone.

I was glad he was sending someone else because I was tired of his ass anyway. Every time he delivered to me, I had to give him a blow job. Although I would have the right amount of cash, he'd refused to give me the product until I do the deed. I contemplated finding another dealer, but it wouldn't be a good look for a firemen's wife to be around asking for drugs. So, I put up with his bullshit instead.

I opened the desk drawer and retrieved the vial. I was down to the last bit, which was why I called David in the first place. After I got my fix, I went to the front of the salon to work on my clients, making sure to take a quick look in the mirror for any residue that may have stuck to my nose.

Lucky for me, the shop closed in a couple of hours, and I could get my "candy."

Just as my last client was leaving, Kevin stopped her.

"Hold on, honey. Let me get this hairpin out of your head," he said, removing it from her hair.

"Why have you been doing that all day?" I asked, placing my hand on my hip.

"Oh, you mean, why I didn't let your clients walk out of here looking a hot mess today? Why I'm saving the reputation of this salon?" He responded with sarcasm.

"I know you're not talking about my work!"

"No, I know you do a great job, but you half-assed today, honey."

"Let me tell you something." I walked towards him, pointing my finger.

Joy stood in between us. "Stop! The both of you," she yelled, keeping us at arm's length. "Now Belinda, I hate to say this, but he's telling the truth. He's caught a few of your customers today who's hair was not on point, and he teased their hair a little here and there to make it right."

"Are you serious?"

"Yes," they both said simultaneously.

Kevin placed his right hand on his hip and pursed his lips. I swear he could be so dramatic at times.

"I'm sorry," I said, apologizing to them both. Honestly, I don't know what I would do without them. It's hard to find people who have your best interest at heart.

Kevin was standing at the door when this tall, caramel brother walked in. He had broad shoulders that tapered down to a slim waist. His arms were muscular and appeared to want to bust out of the form-fitting shirt he was wearing. One thing is for sure. He didn't look like no damn drug dealer, but neither did David.

"Well, okay, caramel, you can give me a sweet tooth any day," Kevin said with a popping of his tongue.

"Hey." I waved him towards me, so he'd know it was me he came to see. "You guys have a good night. See you in the morning," I said, rushing them out the door and locking it behind them.

Standing outside the door, Joy mouthed, who is that? I waved her off and turned my attention to the delivery guy.

"Come with me," I walked toward my office and pulled out one hundred and twenty dollars from my purse. I handed him the money, but he didn't give me the product.

"What are you doing?" I asked, confused by his actions because I'd given him the cash."

A wicked grin came over his face. "David told me you would thank me first."

"Oh, he did, did he? Well, you tell David I said fuck him and fuck you," I spat.

He put the money on the desk and walked away.

"Are you really going to walk away like that?"

He shrugged his shoulders and walked to the front of the salon. "Unlock the door," he ordered.

"No, please, I have the money right here." I tried handing it to him, but he wouldn't take it.

"If you want this, it's going to cost you."

"How much?"

"Three hundred dollars?

"Three hundred dollars!" That's highway robbery!

"Three hundred or nothing," he said calmly.

"Okay, wait a minute," I said, walking back to my office to get the additional money.

I gave him the cash, and he handed me the vial. As I walked around him to unlock the door, he pulled me into his space, pressing me close to his body.

"What the hell are you doing!"

"All of that could be free if you play nice."

"Let me go!" I said, breaking out of his embrace. My heart was beating fast, and my mind was racing a mile a minute.

"Whoa, wait. I'm not going to hurt you, ma. I'm not that type of dude," he said, with his hands in the air. "I'm sorry."

I could hear the sincerity in his voice, and I calmed down. "Don't you ever grab me like that again," I snapped.

He nodded. "I'm really sorry. I just think you are a beautiful woman, and, well, let's just say I got beside myself."

"You damn right about that," I shook my head and sat down in one of the chairs. I gestured for him to have a seat in the chair next to me, in which he obliged. "What's your name?" I asked.

"Geno."

"Well, Geno, nice to meet you," I said, shaking his hand. "I will have to say, you and I started off on the wrong foot, but lucky for you, I'm one who believes in giving second chances."

"Thank you." He smiled.

"You know, for a drug dealer, you have a pleasant disposition about yourself."

"I don't let what I do define who I am."

"Good." I took the vial out of my pocket and took a hit. "So, tell me how old are you, Geno?"

He looked like he was in his mid-twenties, but hell, looks could be deceiving. I'd never seen a drug dealer as nice as him. They were usually about their money, and could care less about anything or anyone -- at least that's how they were portrayed in movies.

He leaned in and whispered in my ear. "Old enough."

The warmth of his breath tickled my neck, causing my pearl to pulsate. "So, you think you can handle all of this, huh?"

He grinned. "I can show you better than I can tell you."

He put his hand on my thigh. After I didn't show any resistance, he leaned over and placed a small kiss on my neck, gradually moving his hand from my thigh up to my breasts. He slid his hand under my shirt and ran his thumb over my erect nipple, causing a tingling sensation to ripple down my spine.

"Let's go to my office," I said, leading the way.

Once in the office, I unzipped his pants, releasing his bulging manhood from the restricting fabric. I dropped to my knees, and slowly took him into my mouth, while I caressed his thickness with my tongue. He let out a loud groan and grabbed the back of my head, pumping deeper into my mouth. I tightened my lips around his shaft, and his pace quickened. I knew it wouldn't be long before he reached his climax. Right when he was on edge, he pulled out of my mouth.

"Stand up," he ordered. When I stood, he knocked everything off the desk and laid me on top of it, "Damn, you feel good," he said as he entered my inner core. He placed my legs on his shoulders, bending them forward as he deepened his strokes. When he was about to reach his orgasm, he pulled out and lowered my legs. "Suck it," he commanded. I got off the desk and dropped to my knees, once again taking him into my mouth until he exploded.

After we cleaned up and got dressed, I walked Geno back to the front of the salon, so he could leave.

"Here you go," he said, handing me the three hundred dollars I had paid him earlier.

I took the money and smiled. "Geno, you can deliver to me any time."

His mouth curled into a smile. He winked and walked out the door.

Autumn

"Thank you," I said, getting out of Antwan's car.

"For what?"

"For inviting me on the trip."

"No, thank you for coming. Because of you, I finally have the complete story, and now I can put this puppy to rest."

Antwan brought my luggage into the house.

"You can put them right there," I said, pointing to the small space next to the staircase.

"Okay." He put the bags down and pulled me into his arms. "I'll see you later, babe." He kissed me.

"Mmmm, see you later." My body tingled from the touch of his hands as they traveled from my lower back, resting on my buttocks. I leaned into him, feeling the thump of his pulsating manhood.

He pulled away. "Look what you've done?" He pointed at the erection growing in his pants. "It would be a shame to waste it," he said with a devilish grin.

I winked. "Well, let's not." I took his hand and led him upstairs.

When we reached the top of the stairs, Gina was walking out of her bedroom.

"Hey, how was your trip?" She asked.

"It was fine. How were things here?"

Antwan, let go of my hand and went into my bedroom, to give us privacy.

"Autumn, it's been crazy. I don't know where to start." She shook her head.

I looked at my bedroom door. I knew Antwan was waiting on me, but Gina's facial expression conveyed I needed to give my attention to her instead. "Give me ten minutes. Let me talk to Antwan, and I will meet you in the den."

She nodded and headed downstairs.

I entered the bedroom, and Antwan was sitting on the bed, fully clothed.

"I know, now is not a good time," he said disappointedly.

"Nope, not at all."

He stood and held me in his arms. "You owe me one," he placed a kiss on my forehead. "Go handle your business. I will see you later.

I escorted him to his car. We shared one last kiss before he left. When I walked into the den, Gina and David were both sitting on the couch.

"Hi David, how are you?" I said, taking a seat on the love seat in front of them.

"Hey," he responded.

"So, tell me, how was everything while I was away?"

"Well, we didn't burn the place down, so I would have to say it was good," he smirked.

"Yeah, everything was good," Gina agreed. She made a gesture with her eyes, signaling we would have to talk later.

I nodded. "So, who's shift is it?"

"It's my shift," David replied. "But there haven't been many calls today, so I'm watching a game."

"Okay, well, I'm going to go unpack," I said, before leaving the two of them.

About twenty minutes later, there was a knock at my door. "Come in."

Gina opened the door and locked it behind her, which I thought was odd, but dismissed it.

"Hey, what's up?" I asked, taking a seat on the bed.

She picked up the chair in the corner of the room and sat next to me.

"Autumn, I think David is dealing drugs in the house."

"What!"

"Shhh, lower your voice."

"What makes you think that he's dealing drugs?"

"Well, I was down in the call center, when I overheard some yelling from upstairs. I cracked the door so that I could hear them better. I overheard David say, "if you fuck up this deal for me, both of you are dead." Then someone screamed out in pain. I quickly closed the door and stayed there until the end of my shift, but I'm telling you, something is not right with him."

She was suspicious, and now, so was I.

"Okay, you let me know if you see or hear anything else."

"Aren't you going to say something to him?"

"No, not yet. I need more evidence."

She nodded. "Okay, will do."

"Where is David now?"

"He went into the call center."

"Okay."

When Gina opened the door to leave my room, David was standing in the hallway. He gave her this chilling look before going into his bedroom. Gina looked back at me nervously, then went to her room and locked the door behind her. So many thoughts crossed my mind, but the fear of the unknown frightened me the most. I have never seen this side of David, and that's what scares me.

Belinda

"Ricky, stop playing and turn the light back on!" I yelled from the shower as I rinsed the soap off my body.

Ricky entered the bathroom. "I didn't turn the lights off."

I turned off the water, opened the shower curtain, and wrapped the towel around me.

"You play too much," I said, stepping out of the tub.

"I'm not playing. I was watching tv when the power went out."

I looked out the window. All our neighbor's lights were on, and suddenly I remembered that I forgot to pay the light bill. When I turned around, Ricky was standing there watching me.

"You forgot to pay the light bill again, didn't you?"

"Yes," I said nonchalantly.

"Belinda, this shit has to stop! We make too much damn money to be getting our lights turned off like this!" He was angry, and he had every right to be. I was slipping, and I mean slipping bad.

"I'll pay it in the morning," I said, walking past him to go get the candles out of the closet.

"Is that all you have to say?"

"Well, what do you want me to say, Ricky? I told you, I'm going to get the lights turned back on in the morning." He was pissing me off with his attitude.

He grabbed his gym bag and started putting clothes in it.

"Where are you going?" I asked.

"To get a room."

"You're doing too much. One night in the dark won't hurt." I undid my towel and let it hit the floor. "Besides, it could be fun."

He continued packing. "Sex isn't going to make this right, Belinda. I'm leaving."

"Well, wait, let me get some clothes on, and I will go with you."

"No, I don't want to be around you right now. Besides, it could be fun," he said sarcastically before walking out of the bedroom. He grabbed his keys off the hook and left. I watched as his car disappeared down the road. After I could no longer see his taillights, I went into the laundry room and grabbed the stash I had hidden. I opened the vial and took a hit. Ah, no worries, I thought as I enjoyed the escape. I slid down to the floor and took another hit. I was on cloud high, and nothing could compare to the way I was feeling at that moment.

I don't remember much outside of getting high that night, but I was awakened by the sound of the dryer, turning the clothes I had placed in there the night before.

I sat up. Why am I naked? I thought as I looked around the room, trying to gain focus. I opened my closed fist, and there lay the empty vial in my hand. I quickly put away all evidence of my addiction. I stood to leave and winced at the pain from sleeping on the floor. I noticed the candle had burned completely, leaving only the small piece of metal used to hold the wick and what was left of the wax. I listened carefully for movement in the house and didn't hear any. I walked out of the laundry room into the living room and looked out the window. Ricky's car wasn't in the driveway. I looked at the clock on the wall. Nine-forty- five! I said, alarmed. I was supposed to be at the shop and hour ago for an eight-thirty appointment. I hurried to the bedroom to get my cell phone. Four missed calls from the salon. I called the shop, and Kevin picked up.

"Where are you?"

It was apparent he looked at the caller Id and saw it was me calling because he didn't bother to say the script we say when answering the phone.

"I'm running late."

"No, you're not running late, you are late," he snapped.

"I know. Do I have any clients waiting on me?"

"No. Your eight-thirty and nine o'clock appointments left. And your ten o'clock canceled."

"Okay, so I'm clear until two. "

"Yeah, but did you forget today is prom. We have four walk-ins, so we need you to get your little fanny down here like two hours ago," he said, matter-of-factly with sarcasm sprinkled over his tone.

"I'll be there in an hour," I said before hanging up the phone.

Next, I called Ricky.

"Hello." He answered.

"Hey, thanks for covering the light bill for me."

"Oh, I didn't cover it for you. I expect you to reimburse me when I get there."

"Where are you?"

"I'm at work."

"Oh, I forgot."

"Well, I'm not surprised, you've seemed to be forgetting a lot lately."

"I got you. Thanks again," I said, ending the call.

The salon was busy, just as Kevin had said. When I walked in the door, Joy and Kevin gave me the side-eye, but I pretended I didn't notice. I put my things away and didn't waste any time jumping in to help them. We worked our fingers to the bone, but when we finished, we had fifteen satisfied young ladies for the prom outside of our regular customers.

I was thankful that we were all beat because I didn't have to hear their mouths about how I'd screwed up lately. I already knew it and needed no confirmation.

Chloe

"Hey babe," Devin said, Kissing me on the cheek. "What you got there?"

"Just going over the seating arrangements for the wedding."

I had spent the last two hours going over details for the reception.

"So, how is it coming?"

"Well, I got our table and our parent's table done. However, I'm trying to find a place to sit your Uncle Joe because everyone can't take his personality."

"Yeah, he most definitely needs to be with someone who can handle him."

"I think Aunt Pat might be the one to keep him in check." I said, as I erased her name from one table and placed it next to Uncle Joe's name."

Devin snapped his fingers. "Hey, what about Millie? She seems to be more like Aunt Pat personality-wise?"

"You're right. Together they will put him in his place."

Uncle Joe could be offensive sometimes with his obscene jokes, but my Aunt Pat and Devin's cousin Millie would surely take care of that. They both could — like the old folks say, "chew you up and spit you out." They took no mess from anyone.

"Can you believe it's only three months before the wedding?" I said excitedly.

"I know." He smiled, tossing the orange he had just gotten out of the fruit tray into his workout bag. "I'm going to the gym." He kissed me on the forehead and left.

I had just finished putting up everything when my cell phone rang. "Hey girl," I said, putting the phone on speaker.

"Hey, has he called you again?" Anna asked.

"No, I haven't heard from him. Why?"

"Geno and I have orders for a drop today. I was curious to know if you were who we were meeting with, that's all."

"Nope, it's not me. Derek hasn't contacted me since I did that drop."

And I was happy he hadn't done so. The less I heard from him, the better. As soon as that thought crossed my mind, the doorbell chimed.

"Hold on, Anna. Someone's at the door."

"Okay, call me back."

"No, stay on the phone," I said, as I watched the tall silhouette standing on the other side of the stained-glass door. "Anna, it's him," I whispered.

"Him, who?"

"Derek!" I whispered.

"What is he doing there?"

"I don't know." I hid behind the counter in the kitchen on the floor so he couldn't see me.

"Don't open the door."

"I'm not."

My heart was pounding, and beads of sweat formed on my forehead. Damn, out of all times to have my blinds open. The next knock on the door was much louder than the first, causing me to jump.

"Is that him knocking?"

"Yes."

He knocked again, then again. Still, I didn't budge from my hiding spot.

"Anna, he's calling me."

"Don't answer it."

"I won't."

Derek called me four times before giving up. I heard him walk away, so I peeped around the counter to make sure he was gone. I didn't see him, so I stood and looked out the window.

"Boo," he said, popping up and startling me. He had hidden below the window pane. I stood frozen as if I had seen a ghost. I could feel the blood draining from my face. The sound of Anna's voice calling my name brought me out of my trance, but I couldn't speak.

He placed his cell phone to his ear and kept his eyes on me. My phone vibrated, indicating that I had an incoming call. He mouthed, answer it.

I knew Anna was still on the phone, so I merged the call and prayed she would be quiet and listen. I was thankful that she did just that.

"Meet me at Echo Park by the swan ride in an hour." He disconnected the call and gave me one last stare before walking away.

I ended the call on my end and called Anna back. "Hey," I said when she answered the phone. "Is Echo Park where you are doing your drop?"

"Nope. So, what's his deal?"

"I don't know. I've told him not to come here."

"Do you want me and Geno to follow you?"

"I would love that, but what about your drop?"

"It's not until later. I'll pick Geno up, and we will be close by. Just pretend you're there by yourself."

"Okay. Thanks, Anna."

"No problem. See you soon."

When I arrived at the location, Derek was standing by the tree. "Let's go for a ride," he said, pointing at the swans.

"No, thank you. I'd rather stay on land."

He lifted the side of his shirt enough for me to see his gun. I nodded my head and walked ahead of him. I sat down in the swan, and he sat next to me. My stomach was in knots, and my mind was in overdrive. He began to paddle the swan away from the dock. When we got out of earshot of the employee and line of customers, he started talking.

"Chloe, you seem not to understand this arrangement you and I have." He looked at me. His eyes were cold, and his face tight. I could see his muscles twitching under his skin. "I have too much riding on you doing what I tell you to do. That means when I call you, you pick up. If I come to your hou-"

"Hold it right there," I said, cutting him off. "That's a problem, I asked you not to come to my house, and you did it anyway. What if my boyfriend saw you?"

"He wouldn't have. I saw him when he left the house."

"Oh, so you're watching my house now?"

"Chloe, stay focused. Listen to what I tell you, and you take this to heart. If you fuck this up…" He lifted his shirt again. "I- will-kill-you." He took the gun from his hip and pointed to my side. "Do you understand?"

I nodded.

"Nah, I want to hear you say it."

"I understand."

"Okay, then let this be the last time we have this conversation."

He paddled us back to the dock and helped me out of the swan. We walked back to the tree, away from everyone else.

"I left a bag in the ceiling of the women's bathroom. I put an out of order sign on the door of the stall. Once you get it, go to Chinatown, there will be a guy waiting for you in front of the Bamboo plaza. He will be wearing a white cap and red sneakers. You will say, "Wǒ" to him, and he will instruct you on what to do next. Any questions?"

"Just one. What does Wǒ mean?

"It means me. It's your code word. Do not forget it." He pulled his sunglasses out of his shirt pocket. "Make sure you are wearing these clothes you have on because he has this description of you."

I nodded.

"And by the way, next time come alone."

He put the sunglasses on his face and walked away.

Anna

Geno and I watched Chloe and Derek's interaction closely. To the naked eye, it would appear there was nothing out of the ordinary, but I knew differently. That's why as soon as he walked away, I called her.

"Hey, are you okay?"

"Yeah, I'm fine. He knew you two were here with me."

"What? Did you tell him we were coming?"

"No, I didn't," I said, annoyed by her accusation.

"Damn, I wonder how he knew?"

"That's a good question. Let me know when you figure it out."

There was a short pause. "Well, I really can't focus on that right now. Geno and I are going to bounce. We have to get ready for business."

"It wouldn't be in Chinatown by chance, would it?"

"Nah, why you ask?

"Because that's where I have to go."

"When?"

"Like now?"

"Damn, I wish we could accompany you, but we have a little drive before we get to our destination."

"Thanks anyway," I said sadly.

"Hey, keep your head up. Remember our talk," she said encouragingly.

"Yeah, well, let me go. I'm running out of time."

"Gotcha. I'll hit you up later, alright."

"Okay."

We arrived at Dream Hollywood and took the elevator to the top floor as we were instructed.

When we walked into the room, to our surprise David was sitting in a chair, and across from him was Derek, whom we both recognized from the park earlier. Geno and I glanced at each other and re-focused our attention back on them.

"Come in." Derek gestured with the wave of his hand. He smiled. "Have a seat. Would you like a drink?"

Neither one of us answered.

"London, fix them a drink," he ordered the doorman. "Give them a double shot of Hennessy."

London did as he was told and brought over our drinks.

"Now, let's get down to business, shall we?" Derek continued.

David sat his drink on the glass coffee table and cleared his throat.

"Um, Derek, this is Geno and Anna." He pointed to each of us as he announced our names.

"Hey, Anna, Geno," Derek gave us each a handshake. The look on his face confirmed that he recognized us.

"These two are my most loyal and trusted workers. They get the job done."

"Is that right?" Derek sat back in his chair and crossed his right leg over his left leg. He sat quietly, eyeing the both of us for what seemed like forever. Geno kept his poker face, and so did I, although my stomach was doing flips, I manage to maintain my composure. His tight lips curved into a smile, and I took a deep breath.

"Relax," he said, before continuing. He told us step by step the details in which we needed to know for the big deal that would be happening two weeks from our meeting. Right before we got ready to leave, he said.

"Anna, I trust you will get Peaches prepared."

"I will," I said, standing.

David looked at me, and I knew he would question me later.

"Geno, I got to get out this game," I said when the elevator doors closed.

"You ain't lying," he agreed. "I'm a small-time dealer. David done pulled us into some shit."

I mused. "Yeah, we got to get out." I had a plan, but I didn't share it with Geno because the less he knew, the better off he would be.

Autumn

I tried on seven outfits before choosing a green sleeveless ruffled shoulder dress. Antwan was on his way to pick me up, so I could meet his parents. I wanted to look nice, and as my aunt would always say, "You will never get a second chance to make a great first impression."

Just as I applied the finishing touches to my make-up, the doorbell chimed. I quickly put the scattered products away, grabbed my purse off the bed, and went downstairs.

"You look beautiful," Antwan said when I opened the door.

"Thank you." I smiled.

"Are you ready?"

"I am." I closed the door behind me and followed Antwan to his car.

"I have to tell you I'm a little nervous about meeting your family, especially your parents."

He reached for my hand and interlocked his fingers with mine.

"Don't worry. They are going to love you."

"I sure hope so." I sighed.

When we arrived at his childhood home, there were several cars in the yard. I closed my eyes and took a couple of deep breaths.

"Relax, it's going to be alright," he smiled.

We entered the house through the kitchen. It was beautifully decorated with a vineyard theme. There was an array of wine bottles lined atop the cabinets with a grapevine, that appeared to wrap around each one. There were also pictures of chefs and vineyards on the walls. His mother really had a great taste in design.

"Mom, this is Autumn. Autumn, this is my mom, Lena."

"Hi, Mrs. Lena." I smiled.

"Hello, Autumn, nice to meet you," she said as she retrieved the pie from the oven. "You two are right on time. Dinner will be ready in a few minutes." She smiled.

"Can I help you with anything?"

"Oh, no, honey, I have it, thank you though." She smiled again. "I like this one."

"Me, too." Antwan winked.

He took my hand and led me through the dining room into a large living room, where the rest of the family were watching tv.

"Hey, everyone," Antwan said when we entered the room.

They all greeted us with their versions of hello. His dad was the first to stand.

"Dad, this is Autumn. Autumn, this is my dad, William."

"Hi," I said shyly, as all eyes were on me.

His dad smiled. "Hi, Autumn, I'm glad you could join us."

"Thank you for having me."

Antwan introduced each family member one by one. They were all kind and welcomed me with warm hearts.

Shortly after we settled, his mom announced dinner was ready, so we all took our respectful seats at the dinner table. It was decorated with fresh floral arrangements, and a variety of food in gourmet dishes sat in between them.

"Everything looks delicious, Lena," his aunt Lisa commented.

As if on cue, everyone agreed.

"Well, I hope you all enjoy it." She smiled. "Dig in."

We were halfway through dinner when the conversation became about me.

"So, Autumn, are you from LA?" his mother asked.

"No, ma'am. I'm from Missouri."

"Oh, what part?"

"St. Louis?"

"Really? We grew up in East St. Louis." His aunt chimed in. "Just right across the river. We had some good times back then." She mused.

"We sure did. Who are some of your people, we may know them?" Mrs. Lena asked.

"Well, I was raised by my aunt Mattie."

"What's her last name?"

"Graham."

"That name sounds familiar; did she bake cakes? His aunt asked. "I remember there was a Ms. Mattie that baked cakes for that Sister Soul restaurant." She reflected.

I shook my head. "No. She didn't do much baking. She was a nurse."

"Oh, okay. So, what's your mother's name?"

"Her name was Sharon Taylor, but she's deceased."

"Aw, I'm sorry to hear that," both his aunt and mom said simultaneously.

Antwan eyed both of them. "That's enough questions, don't you think?"

"Antwan, we are only trying to get to know her, and how else are we going to do that, if we don't ask questions?" His mom responded.

I touched him on his arm. "It's okay."

"Thank you," his mom said, before taking a sip of her wine.

"So, what's your dad's name?" his aunt asked.

"My dad's name is Joseph Rivera, and he's also deceased."

His mom began coughing.

"Lena, are you alright?" Mr. William asked, patting her on the back.

"Yeah, I got strangled," she managed to say in between coughs. When her coughs subsided, she stood.

"Excuse me. William, can I see you for a minute?" She walked towards the far-end of the house. Mr. William followed behind her.

We finished our dinner, and everyone left, except Antwan and me. We started clearing the table and cleaning the kitchen.

"Do you think your mom is okay?"

"I'm sure she is, but I'll check on her after we're done with the dishes."

Shortly after, his mom came into the kitchen. "Sorry about earlier, leave those dishes, I'll finish cleaning them later. Come," she said as she walked into the dining room. She sat down at the table, "Come sit down." She gestured, and Antwan and I sat across from her. She gently stroked the black box in front of her.

"Here you go." Mr. William handed her a glass of wine. "Would you two like some?" he asked.

"No, thank you." We both said.

"Mom, not the baby pictures again," Antwan protested.

She ignored his comment. It's funny how men transform into little boys when they are in the presence of their mother.

"Listen, I don't know how else to say this, so I'm just going to say it." She looked at Mr. William, and he nodded.

"Go ahead, honey," he prompted.

She took a deep breath and nodded back at him. "You two are brother and sister."

Antwan and I looked at each other like 'did we hear her correctly?'

"Mom, repeat what you just said."

"Baby listen, I'm-"

He interrupted her. "Nah, Ma, repeat what you said!" His voice was rising to another octave.

"She is your sister Antwan."

I sat in dismay, at a loss for words. It was like a black cloud that had consumed me.

"What the fuck, Ma!" Antwan screamed.

"Son, calm down." Mr. Williams interjected. "That's your mother, show some respect."

"Did you know about this?" Antwan asked Mr. Williams. He didn't answer but held his head down.

"How could ya'll do this shit to me, to us!" He yelled.

Tears ran down my face, my chest tightened, and I couldn't breathe.

"I didn't know you were dating her, Antwan. Please, let me explain," she pleaded.

"Explain what, Ma! My whole life has been a damn lie." He paced back and forward. "And you're not my dad! What the fuck!"

"Antwan, I was young. Your father has only seen you twice since you were born. Once after I birthed you and the last, when you were a little over a year old. After that visit, he never contacted me again, and I never reached out to his family. You were two when William and I met. When you were three years old, William, um your dad and I got married. He adopted you, and we moved out here."

"That's no excuse. You should have told me!" He snapped.

I couldn't take it anymore. I felt like I was suffocating and needed to get out of there.

"Take me home, please."

Antwan wiped his tears. He pulled his keys out of his pocket. "Let's go."

"Please don't leave. You shouldn't be driving like this." Mrs. Lena tried to grab his arm, but he snatched away.

I could hear her crying in the distance, as he closed the door behind us.

We were both subdued on the way to my house. When he pulled into the drive, I quickly unfastened my seatbelt to get out of the car, but he placed his hand on my arm to stop me.

"Wait." He switched the engine off. "Autumn, we have to talk about this."

"What do you want me to say, Antwan? I mean, you're my brother! You and I have done things brothers and sisters shouldn't do!"

Tears rolled down my face.

"Autumn, we didn't know."

"Yeah, but it's still not right!"

He tried to hug me, but I moved out of his reach. "I have to go."

"Listen, I'm going to talk to my mom and get more clarity about this."

"Yeah, you do that." I opened the car door. "I need some time to think." I shut the door and walked away.

When I got to my bedroom, I looked out the window to see if Antwan had left, and to my surprise, he was still parked in the driveway. While I stood there watching him, my cell phone rang.

"Hello," I answered.

"Let's take a DNA test," Antwan suggested.

"Okay," I agreed, before hanging up the phone.

I watched as Antwan backed out of the drive. Then, I sat on the bed and called Mercedes. At the sound of her voice, I lost it and started crying hysterically.

"Autumn, honey, what's wrong?" She asked, with her voice on the verge of panic.

I tried to explain, but couldn't form the words from the sobbing.

"Autumn, whatever it is, it's going to be alright."

"No, it's not." I blew my nose and tried to get myself together.

Mercedes waited quietly while I went through my meltdown. "Are you okay now to tell me what's happened?"

"Antwan is my brother!" I blurted out and started back crying.

"He's what? How? When?"

"I went to meet his parents today, and his mother told us we were siblings. Oh, Mercedes, everything is just so-"

"Calm down, honey. It's going to be okay."

"You don't understand. I slept with my brother."

She didn't respond.

"Hello," I said, making sure she was still on the line.

"Autumn, this is not your fault. Don't beat yourself up about this. The first thing I'm going to recommend is the two of you get a DNA test."

"We are." I sniffled.

"Okay, good. Now listen to me. No matter what the results are, it will be okay."

"Mercedes, if he's my brother, I don't think I could live with that."

"Autumn don't talk like that. You are a strong young lady. You will get through this," she assured me.

We talked a little longer. It was not until she had me laughing that she ended our conversation.

The following day, Antwan and I met at the Health facility for DNA testing.

We both filled out the paperwork required before the test could be administered. We were called to the back, and blood was drawn as well as a swab of the mouth at our request. Afterward, we were informed it would take a week minimum before we get the results back.

"Do you want to go somewhere and talk?" Antwan asked as we walked to our cars.

"No, I think we need to wait until we get the results back, so we can know how to proceed," I said, opening my car door and sitting down. "Bye, Antwan." I started the engine, put the car in gear, and drove away.

I cried all the way home. Having to wait a week seemed like waiting an eternity to me.

Antwan respected my wishes and didn't contact me the entire week. On the day the results came in, he asked me to meet him at his place so that we could open the envelope together.

When I walked into his apartment, instantly, I was reminded of the day we made love, and I began to feel sick. My heart sunk, and my anxiety skyrocketed. Sweat began to form on my forehead, and I felt faint. Antwan assisted me to the couch.

"Are you alright?" He asked.

I shook my head, no.

"Would you like a glass of water?"

"Yes. And a glass of wine, please." He hurried and brought me back the water, but no wine.

"Take some deep breaths," he instructed.

It took a few minutes, but I soon calmed down.

"I'll be right back." He walked into his bedroom and returned with the envelope in hand. "Do you want me to read it, or do you want to?"

"You read it."

He looked at me with uncertainty in his eyes. Then he opened the envelope. His eyes scanned the paper.

"What does it say?"

He handed me the document and sat quietly as I read the results. "Oh my God, oh my God. I'm going to be sick," I said as I ran to the bathroom, locking the door behind me. I vomited until I had nothing left to throw up. After that, I sat on the toilet and cried hysterically. Antwan was my brother, and I wanted to die. At that moment, if he had a window in the bathroom, I would have jumped out of it.

"Autumn, open the door."

"No, go away!"

"I'm not going anywhere. Please talk to me," he pleaded.

I didn't respond. I just continued to cry. I don't know how long I was in that bathroom, but when I walked out, he was sitting on the floor next to the door. I walked past him, and he quickly stood up and followed me. I grabbed my purse off the couch and opened the door, but he pushed it shut.

"We need to talk."

"I don't want to talk."

"Autumn, this is not just going to go away."

"Let me go, please."

He watched as I stood with my arms folded. He sighed and stepped aside.

"I'll be here when you're ready to talk."

Without saying a word, I opened the door and left.

As I drove home, I thought about a lot of things like how Mercedes and McKenzie were MJ's birth parents. Antwan had his parents. And I had no one. Well, I had Mercedes and McKenzie, but they weren't my biological parents, and for the first time in a long time, I felt alone. Tears began to roll down my face.

By the time I got home, I had decided to end it all. I walked upstairs to my room and closed the door. I reached into my closet and got the bottle of pills I had stolen from David earlier and the bottle of vodka I stored with it. After consuming the pills and alcohol, I pulled a small notepad and pen out of my bedside drawer and jotted down.

"Ask Antwan." I laid it next to me as I waited to slip into a deep sleep, never to awaken again.

My body was getting heavy, and I knew time was drawing near. I was ready to meet my maker. I wanted out of this life. It was full of pain and sorrow and one disappointment after another. I heard my bedroom door open, but I couldn't move.

"Autumn! What have you done?" Gina panicked.

I loved Gina. She's a beautiful person inside and out. She's always caring for others. I could hear her talking to someone, but couldn't understand what they were saying. I don't know how long it had been since I heard Gina's voice, but soon I felt hands all over me. "NO, just let me go in peace!" I screamed, but no one heard me. "Ouch! That hurt. Please leave me alone." I pleaded, but they didn't seem to care about my pleas.

Suddenly, I didn't hear anyone or anything. I was gone. I was free. It was as though I had an out-of-body experience. I could see a man pounding on my chest.

"Come on! Come On!" He repeated, his voice full of panic.

"Give her another shot of Narcan," he ordered.

I watched as they worked vigorously to bring me back. But I didn't want to come back. I wanted to go.

However, God had other plans. When he injected the medicine in my arm, my heart began to beat.

"We have a heartbeat," he announced. He took a moment to wipe a tear from his eye. "Good job, man," he said, as he bumped fist with his co-worker.

And like that, I was back. I could hear the sound of paper ripping and feel the bandages being used, but I couldn't move. A tear escaped my right eye, and I felt it roll down the side of my face. I was saddened that they had brought me back. They didn't understand my pain, and they never would.

Belinda

"So, do you want to play?" Geno raised his eyebrows while dangling the two vials of substance in front of me.

"Hell, no! Just give me my shit," I snapped, snatching the two vials out his hand. Truth is the sex was good — real good — but it was almost that time of the month, and I was cramping. Plus, I had to open the salon in thirty minutes, so I just wanted to get a couple of hits before we opened for business.

Geno chuckled and shook his head. "It's all good, ma. Here's a little something for later." He handed me another vial. "I'll be busy the next couple of days, so pace yourself. I'll cash in on it later." He winked before leaving.

I locked the door behind him and went to my office. I opened one of the vials and rubbed the substance across my gums. Then I pulled a syringe out of the drawer. I had never used by a syringe, but I saw it in a movie and wanted to give it a try. After it was ready, I injected it in my arm, and immediately my heart began to beat rapidly, as though it was coming out of my chest. I started to panic and tried to stand. But I fell on the floor shaking all over, then I collapsed.

I don't know how long I was out, but I heard Kevin yelling call nine-one-one.

I tried to move, but I couldn't. My body felt too heavy like someone was sitting on me. I tried to speak, and no words would come out. So, I prayed. Lord, please don't let me die. I promise I will get help. By the time the ambulance arrived, I was slipping in and out of consciousness. I remember being lifted into the ambulance.

The next time I awoke, I was lying in a hospital bed with Ricky by my bedside.

"Hey," he said when I opened my eyes.

He pressed the nurse button on the side of the bed.

"Hey." I smiled.

A look of concern covered his face. "You gave us a scare."

The nurse entered the room. "Hi, how do you feel?" She asked, checking my vitals.

"I'm good."

She nodded her head.

"The doctor will be in to see you shortly. Is there anything I can get you?"

"No, I'm fine."

"Okay, well, just push the button if you need me." She closed the door behind her.

I could see the questions in Ricky's eyes, but he reframed from asking. Instead, he climbed in bed with me and held me in his arms.

Shortly, there was a knock on the door; it was Kevin and Joy.

"Hey, I'm glad to see you awake," Kevin said as he entered first.

"How are you?" Joy asked.

"I'm doing fine."

"Girl, you scared the hell out of me. I didn't know what to think when I saw you lying on that floor," Kevin expressed.

"I know, I'm sorry, guys."

"So, when are they releasing you?" Joy asked.

Before I could answer, Dr. Mathis knocked on the door and entered. "Hello everyone," she said, looking around the room at each of us.

"Hi," we all responded in unison.

"How are you feeling?" she asked.

"I'm fine."

"Great." She smiled and looked at Ricky lying next to me. "So, I think we need to talk about some things before you are released."

I nodded.

"Privately," She said, looking around the room.

"It's okay. You can speak in front of them, their family." I smiled.

She touched my hand, and with a nod of her head, she continued.

"You were lucky. The cocaine you injected was laced with Fentanyl, which is an opioid used to treat people with severe pain. Many times, it's given to patients after they've had surgery. You could have died, Mrs. Lane."

She paused before she continued. No doubt, it was to give me time to consume what she was saying. I sat quietly, mainly because I was at a loss for words.

"I recommend rehab to get you on a path to sobriety. I hope you will accept," she said, waiting for an answer. I looked around, and all eyes were on me, but what they didn't know was I had made a promise to God. He had spared my life, and for that, I owed him.

"Yes, I will go."

Ricky kissed me on my forehead. Kevin and Joy breathe a sigh of relief, and Dr. Mathis smiled.

"Great, we will see if we can find a facility with a vacancy." She patted my hand and left.

"Don't worry about the salon. We got you covered," Kevin said.

"I agree," Joy added.

"I'm proud of you, babe. I'll be here to support you any way I can," Ricky said as he held me close.

At that moment, I truly felt loved. No matter what it took, I was determined to kick my drug habit and get my life back on track.

Chloe

Two weeks later

"Derek called me about the big meeting, aka a big drop," I said to Anna, who was on the other end of the phone.

"Yeah, what did he say?"

"He told me to meet him at the warehouse at seven o'clock."

"Really," she said with a hint of doubt in her voice. Well, we were told to be there at eight, so I wonder why the different time."

Now, she had me wondering about the same thing.

"I tell you what, you go. Me, Geno, and Ty will stake out the area."

"I don't want you guys to get in trouble."

"You let us worry about that; plus, I don't trust Derek."

"Yeah, me either."

We talked a little longer before ending the call. I looked at the clock. Six hours till showtime. I busied around the house until two hours before the time for me to leave. I picked out the clothes I would be wearing for this eventful evening. I grabbed a pair of jeans, a dark, loose-fitting shirt so I could conceal my gun and a pair of black sneakers just in case I had to run. When I opened the door to leave, I saw Derek parked across the street.

I walked over to his car. "Why are you here? I've asked you not to come here anymore," I said, feeling annoyed.

"I'm here to pick you up."

I shook my head. "Oh, no! I'm driving myself."

Pulling the gun from the side of his seat, he ordered me to get into the car. I opened the door and sat down. I could feel my weapon poking me in my lower back. I wanted so badly to remove it, but I couldn't risk him knowing I had it.

"Why can't I drive myself?" I asked. One thing I knew about Derek is everything he did was calculated. He glanced over at me and focused back on the road without giving a response.

"Are you going to answer me?"

He took a deep breath. "Just chill Peaches."

I laid my head against the headrest and looked out of the window. He drove for an hour before he pulled over on the side of the road.

"Here, put this on," he said, handing me a sleeping mask.

"No, please don't." I pleaded.

"I'm not going to hurt you. I just don't need you to see where we are going?"

"But you already gave me the address," I refuted.

"No, I gave you an address, but it wasn't this address."

How stupid could I be? I didn't even check to see where the address was. I figured I would put it in my GPS when I was on my way. I took the mask and held it to my face.

"Wait, hand me your phone," he said, holding his hand out for it. When I gave it to him, he turned the location off and threw it out the window.

"Not my phone," I groaned.

"You can get another one when this is all over. Put on the mask."

I did as I was told, then he instructed me to turn my head and face him. He tied a scarf around my face.

"It's not too tight, is it?"

"No."

He put the car in gear. I could tell when he pulled off that he made a U-turn heading back the way we came. He drove about thirty minutes before making a left turn. He drove a little while and turned again. I assume all of this was to confuse me with our whereabouts.

When he finally stopped. He untied the scarf and removed the mask from my face.

We were parked in front of a large warehouse. He typed a code on his phone, and the door began to rise. There was a tall, muscular guy standing at the entrance with a machine gun strapped across his shoulder. I took a mental snapshot of him and the building, something I had learned from Devin. He would say, 'Always pay attention to your surroundings.' After Derek pulled his car inside, he told the guy to go stand his post. He nodded and disappeared.

The inside of the building had another car and a moving van inside.

"Why do you have these vehicles here?" I asked.

"You know Peaches, you sure ask a lot of damn questions?"

"Sorry, Geez, touchy," I said, walking over to read the fine print on the white moving van. It read Joe's Furniture. 'We sell and buy used furniture.'

He leaned on the hood of his car. "You know what I have a question for you? Why didn't you come to visit me? Or even write."

"Derek, we've been over this. I was only sixteen when that happened. I was young. I didn't know how to handle all of that."

"Okay, but why didn't you write me back? I sent you plenty of letters."

"Derek, I didn't get any letters. I swear I didn't." I held my hands up.

"Yeah, I know, you say you didn't get any letters." He mocked.

"You know I never stopped thinking about you, Peaches? Let's try again," he said as he walked over and tried to kiss me. I stepped out of the way. "Oh, so a brother can't get a kiss?"

"No, I told you I am engaged."

"So, what he doesn't know won't hurt him." He pulled me into his arms, and I tried to push him away, but he held on tight. He pushed me against the truck and grabbed my jaw, forcefully kissing me on the mouth. I bit his lip, and he slapped me. He pinned me against the car. I struggled to get away but couldn't. I tried to scream, and he covered my mouth with his hand. I reached for my gun. When I pulled it out, Derek grabbed my arm and twisted it until I dropped the weapon.

"Really, Peaches! You're going to pull a gun on me after all I've done for you!"

He started choking me. I clawed at his face and neck, but it didn't faze him. It seemed the more I tried to fight back, the harder he gripped my throat. Suddenly out of nowhere, I heard a gunshot, and Derek fell to the ground. I looked down at his lifeless body lying there in a pool of blood. I turned to see who had come to my rescue.

"Thank you," I said as I ran into his arms.

Anna

On our way to the address we were given just days before, David called and informed Geno the location had changed.

"Yeah, I got it," Geno said as he hung up the phone. He turned around. "The location has changed."

"What?" I asked.

"What kind of shit is that!" Ty exclaimed.

I shook my head. "I don't like this."

"Yeah, me either," Geno agreed.

Ty sat in the back, continuing his tantrum until Geno pulled the car over on the side of the road.

"Listen, man. I'm a need you to calm the fuck down! This is not the time to be having a fit. I need your head in the game. You feel me." Geno said matter-of-factly.

"Yeah, I feel you. This shit still fucked up, though," Ty responded.

When we arrived at the warehouse, there were no vehicles around, and I got this eerie feeling something wasn't right. When we stepped out of the car, we heard a scream.

"That's Chloe!" I yelled.

Ty ran inside the building, and Geno and I ran behind him. Before we could make it into the building, Ty had pulled his gun and shot Derek in the head. Chloe ran into his arms, sobbing. Suddenly, there was another gunshot. Ty dropped to his knees, and Chloe screamed. Geno and I turned to look behind us. There stood this tall guy with his gun still drawn.

"Get over there," he commanded, pointing to the wall. "Take all of your weapons and put them on the floor." He observed.

"I don't have any," Chloe responded, raising her hands in the air. He nodded and turned his attention back to Geno and me. Once we put our guns on the floor, he instructed us to kick them over to him, and we did. He then had us to face the wall and patted each of us down one by one, beginning with Chloe.

Ty was still alive, but barely. He coughed up blood and moaned in pain. He was dying, and there was nothing we could do to help him.

Once he finished his body search, he walked over to Ty and pulled the trigger. There was silence. Ty's life was ended with a fatal gunshot wound to his head. I covered my mouth and stifled my cry. Sure, I had threatened to kill him myself. I had even gone as far as buying a gun, but it was something about this situation that made me mourn the loss of him. Geno held me in his arms, and I buried my face in his chest.

The guy then pointed his gun at the three of us.

"Hey!" He said, bringing my sobs to a halt. "You three, get over here and pull these bodies on the other side of that moving van."

We stood there as if we were trying to comprehend what he said.

"Now!" He yelled.

We quickly got our asses in gear and did as he instructed. Just when we finished hiding the bodies, a black box truck pulled into the warehouse, and men jumped out with guns.

"Get your hands up!" They yelled. "Get 'um up!" They pointed guns at all of us.

We were handcuffed and lined up against the wall. We watched as they took pictures of the scene. Taped off sections and drew circles around the discovered bodies with chalk. The scene played out like something you would see in a movie.

They transported each of us to the county jail in different cars. When we got there, we were placed in separate cells waiting to be investigated.

Meanwhile back at Fantasy

Gina opened the door.

"Hello, I'm Lieutenant Garrison. Is David Williams here?"

"Yes, he's here." She stepped aside so the officers could come in. "It takes this many, huh?" She said sarcastically as the six men entered the home.

"Where is he?" Lt. Garrison asked, dismissing her comment.

"Follow me."

She led them down to the call center where David was enjoying a football game on television. The men rushed in and apprehended him. Then he was handcuffed and escorted upstairs. The Lieutenant turned to the officers.

"Search this place from top to bottom. Every nook and cranny." He motioned his hand to put emphasis on what he was saying. The officers acknowledged him with a nod and began their search. They started on the top floor — two in David's bedroom, two in Autumn's bedroom, and two in mine.

They worked their way down to the second floor. About forty minutes into their search, an officer shouted from the guest bathroom.

"I found it!"

He pulled brick after brick from under the sink. David had cut a hole in the wall and stored it there, which was the perfect hiding place from us since we didn't use that bathroom.

Lieutenant Garrison looked at me. "Ma'am, I'm going to have to take you down to the station, too."

"Why? That's not mine," she retorted.

He shrugged. "I believe you, but we have to bring everyone in for questioning so we can get to the bottom of this."

"Okay," she said, not putting up a fight.

"Turn around for me, please." One of the officers said as he took the handcuffs out of the pouch, and placed them around her wrists. He escorted her out of the house and put her in a patrol car.

Gina and David were transported to jail, while the officers continued to search the home.

Chloe

The door opened to the holding cell, and Devin walked through. "You did good, babe," he said, wrapping his arms around me.

"Devin, I was so scared."

"I know you were, but it's all over now."

"I sure hope so. Where is Anna?"

"She's in the holding cell."

"Is she alright?"

"Yes."

"When can we leave?"

"They've just brought David and Gina in so-"

"Gina?"

"Yeah, but we know she had nothing to do with it. It's a formality to make sure we have all bases covered. She won't be booked but held in a cell the same as you and Anna until we get him booked in and taken to the back," he explained.

"I understand."

He kissed me. "Hold tight, and we will have you all out of here in a little bit, okay."

"Okay."

After Devin left, I sat there a few minutes before the door opened again.

"Gina," I said, giving her a hug.

"Chloe, what are you doing here?" She asked.

"It's a long story, but why are you here?" I played it off.

"The drug team came in and busted David for drugs, but because he had them hidden in the house, I had to come, too. Chloe, you know I don't mess with drugs in no shape, form, or fashion."

"I know. They will clear all of this up, and you will be out of here before you know it." Changing the subject, I asked. "How is Autumn doing?"

Gina shook her head. "She's still in the hospital.

"Well, I hope she gets better soon. It's all so sad."

Gina sighed. "Yeah, I didn't know she was having any problems."

I sat on my hands and swung my feet as I thought about what Gina said. Autumn was filling Destini shoes, and I know first-hand how Fantasy could be a lot on a person.

"Chloe."

The door opened, and Anna walked in. We both stood to hug her.

"Gina, what are you doing here?" She asked after our little reunion.

"Girl, David was selling drugs out of the house, and they found a large amount he was hiding in the guest bathroom."

"Okay, but what does that have to do with you?"

"The Lieutenant said they had to bring me in too because I live there. But they are not going to charge me."

"Good," Anna took a seat on the bench. "How much longer do we have to be in here?"

"I was wondering the same thing," I responded.

We sat and talked about Autumn, Fantasy, the drug bust, and where we were all going from here.

"I've decided to leave LA," Gina announced.

"Yeah, I've been thinking the same thing," Anna confessed.

"Really," I said sadly, but I understood. Too much had happened. Things were not the same at Fantasy, truth be told, it was time to shut it down.

"Do you think Autumn will keep Fantasy?" I asked.

Gina shook her head. "No. Not after all that's been going on. Plus, the owners are selling the house."

We sat in silence after hearing that news. I'm quite sure we were each reflecting on the time we spent there. It hadn't always been bad. A matter-of-fact, in the beginning, it was good. Many of us got through school with the income made from the call center, and it prevented us from having to struggle financially, as most college students do.

"I'm really going to miss you two, but I understand, and I want nothing but the best for you," I said, breaking the silence.

Anna hugged me. "I'm going to miss you too, Chloe."

"And I'm going to miss you, Anna," Gina said.

Gina and I weren't friends, but I knew her through Anna.

The door opened, and Devin stepped in. "You ladies ready to get out of here."

"Yes!" we said in unison.

He laughed and stepped aside as we walked out. He escorted us to the parking lot and handed me the keys to his car. He pulled me close in an embrace and kissed me gently on the lips. "I'll see you later, drive carefully."

"I love you," I said as he walked away.

"Love you, too."

I gave Anna and Gina a ride home. When we pulled up to the house, I got out also. I wanted one last look at Fantasy before the doors were closed for good. It still looked the same as it did the first day I arrived there for an interview, except instead of shedding leaves, the huge magnolia tree was in full bloom.

"My goodness, look at the mess," I said when we entered the house.

"Yeah, they just threw stuff everywhere," Gina said.

Anna walked into her room. "Now, they didn't have to throw my shit around like this!"

I shook my head at the damaged furniture, clothes, and other items covering the floors as we continued from one room to the next.

"I'm going down to the call center," I said, heading in that direction.

When I opened the door, I looked around the room. Not much had changed since I was here. I stood behind the desk and saw the list of questions still taped near the phone. I walked over to each of the small rooms aligned the wall, and they each still had the red telephones plugged into the wall. It was a bittersweet moment, but I knew it was best for everyone involved.

"Bye, Fantasy," I said, exiting the room.

I found Gina and Anna each in their rooms, packing their things.

"I see you two aren't wasting any time."

"No, ma'am, Anna responded. "I will be hitting the road in the morning. I'm going by the hospital to see Autumn before I leave. Then I'm out of here."

"Me too." Gina agreed.

"Okay, well, I'm out, ladies." I gave them both a hug. I'll see you before you leave right." I said, looking at Anna.

"Yes, I'll stop by." She nodded.

I smiled and headed home.

Anna

While sitting in that jail cell, I decided I was leaving LA and moving back home. I knew this was not the life for me. So, this morning I said my goodbyes to Gina and went to see Autumn. Sadly, not much had changed, but the doctors assured McKenzie and Mercedes that she would recover just fine. They wanted to give her body time to rest after what she went through. So, they kept her sedated.

After leaving the hospital, I stopped by to see Chloe and Devin.

"Good morning," Chloe said when she opened the door.

"Good morning, Chloe." I hugged her and took a seat in the living room. Devin came out shortly and joined us. The three of us talked about the events that had taken place less than twenty-four hours ago.

"Devin, how did you know where we were? David had called us while we were on our way to the location, I gave you, and had sent us to a different place."

"Ah, I never trust drug dealers and especially when my babe is involved," he said, interlocking his fingers with Chloe's. "I put a tracer in her shoe."

Chloe's mouth fell open. "Really! but when?"

He smiled. "Why do you think I told you to wear those shoes?"

"Whew, I'm just glad she listened," I said, and we all laughed.

"So, what are you trying to say?" She tossed one of the decorative pillows at me.

"You know you can be hard-headed sometimes, Chloe."

"Yeah, whatever, I'm not hard-headed," she countered.

"Yeah, you kinda are." Devin agreed, and we both laughed. Chloe tightened her lips.

"Well, guys, I better hit the road. I'll see you on the east coast." I smiled.

"That's right. Two months to go, and I will be Mrs. Devin Johnson." She leaned her head on Devin's shoulder.

"Thanks for everything, Devin."

He nodded. "Take care of yourself."

"I will."

Before getting on the highway, I made one last stop. I had to say goodbye to my boy Geno. When I pulled up to his apartment, he was sitting on the steps. I smiled and shook my head. I'm going to miss this guy. I thought as I got out of the car, and he wrapped his arms around me.

"What's up!" He held me tight in his embrace.

"I'm leaving LA."

"What? For good?" He held me at arm's length to see my face.

I nodded. "For good."

"Ah, man," he said disappointedly. "I understand, do what you have to do, shorty," He smiled.

"You, too. I'm going to miss you."

"Imma miss you too. You be good."

We gave each other one last hug, and I left.

Geno never knew that Chloe and I told Devin about the big drop, which is why the operation failed. I told Devin that Geno would be with us, and he was a good guy. So, like us, he wasn't charged. I didn't know if he would truly get out of the game, but what I did know was that he'd been given a second chance to get himself right.

When I turned onto the interstate, I looked in my rearview mirror. "Goodbye, LA. Goodbye," I said as I headed home.

Autumn

I opened my eyes and saw Mercedes sitting next to my bed. "Hi, sweetheart," she said.

McKenzie stood and walked over to my bed. "Hi, pumpkin." He kissed me on the cheek. "How are you feeling?"

"I'm okay. How did you guys-"

Mercedes touched my face. "Your friend Gina called us." She smiled.

"I'm going to go get the nurse," McKenzie said while walking toward the door. A couple of minutes later, he was back with the doctor.

"Hi, Autumn, I'm Dr. Roberts."

"Hi."

"How are you feeling?"

"I'm fine."

"I'm going to check your breathing."

I nodded, and he proceeded to do so. After he checked my vitals, we discussed the next course of action, which included me getting some counseling once I was released from the hospital. When the doctor left, McKenzie said, "Autumn, Mercedes, and I have been talking, and we think you should come home with us."

Mercedes nodded her head in agreement.

"Uh, I don't know, I have a lot to do here."

"No, you don't," McKenzie replied matter-of-factly. "You are coming home with us."

Mercedes looked at him but didn't give a rebuttal. She handed me two envelopes. One had Gina's name on it, and the other was from Anna.

"I'll read them later." I handed the letters to McKenzie, and he placed them on the table positioned at the foot of the bed.

"Autumn, what happened? Why did you do this?" He asked.

I sighed. "Did you see Antwan?"

"Yes, we did, and he told us it would be best if we heard it from you."

I looked at Mercedes. She smiled and nodded her head, which gave me the courage to tell them.

"Antwan and I are brother and sister."

McKenzie sat up straight. Mercedes took a deep breath. "Is that why you did this?" She asked.

A tear escaped my eye, and she wiped it away. "Sweetheart, there is nothing in this world worth you taking your life over."

"Autumn, death is a final solution to a temporary problem," McKenzie said.

"He's right," Mercedes agreed. "Don't you know how hurt we were to see you like this? We love you, and you are a big part of our family." She rubbed my head.

Tears begin rolling down my face. "I love you, guys, too."

Later that evening, I looked at the envelopes sitting on the table and picked them up. I decided to read Gina's first.

Autumn,

I want to thank you for everything you've done for me. You are a great friend, and I am glad to have you in my life. I have decided to move back home. I feel it's best for me at this time.

My suspicions of David were correct. He was dealing drugs, and right out of Fantasy. Yep, right under our noses. The law did a drug bust at our place, and he was arrested. It's a long story, and I will have to share it with you when you wake up.

The house is in a mess. Things were thrown all over the place during the drug search. I boxed all of your clothes and labeled the boxes for you.

I will talk to you soon.

Love,

Gina

*P.s. The key is in the envelope.

Next, I picked up the envelope from Anna. She, too, had sealed her key with her letter.

Autumn,

So much has transpired since you have been in the hospital. There is a lot to tell you, but it will have to wait until you are awake.

However, due to the turns of events, I have decided to leave L.A. and go back home.

I hope you have a speedy recovery, and I wish you all the best. I will check on you soon.

Anna

I laid my head back on the pillow. The truth was that I knew deep down it was time for me to move on, too. I looked over at Mercedes and McKenzie and smiled as I watched them both napping on the small couch. I'm going back to Chicago. I thought to myself as I smiled and drifted off to sleep.

I was in the hospital another two days before the doctor released me. During that time, McKenzie had mailed all of my clothes to Chicago and had the property cleaned.

Entering the house was very sad for me. All of the furniture was gone, and it was just an empty space. McKenzie explained that the owners were selling the house, so everything had to go. We walked down to what was the call center. To my surprise, the desk was still there, but the pictures were off the wall. I looked in each office, and they were empty except for the last one.

In the corner sat a red phone on the floor. I opened the door and smiled as I held it in my hand.

"Are you ready?" McKenzie asked.

I nodded. We walked back outside. On the way to the car, I stopped and turned around, taking one final look at the house. McKenzie wrapped his arm around my shoulders. "Let's go home."

Epilogue

Six months later

Chloe

I was officially Mrs. Devin Johnson, and I couldn't be happier. We were married in Miami two months after the whole drug bust operation.

After returning from our honeymoon in Dubai, we decided to relocate to Miami. Devin is working with the Miami DEA.

As for me, I'm still searching for that perfect job. In the meantime, I have enrolled at the University of Miami to get my master's degree in Psychology and will begin this fall. I talked to Anna and Belinda often. Anna has also gone back to school to get a nursing degree, and Belinda has been six months clean. She said some days it's a battle, but she is determined to overcome it. She has an excellent support team there. Ricky, Joy, and Kevin have continued to encourage and motivate her each day.

Autumn

Since being back in Chicago, I have been going to counseling. It took some time for me to forgive myself and let go of the shame. I realized it was our parent's lies and deceit that caused this problem. We were merely victims in this whole situation.

I reached out to Antwan three months ago, and he has visited me twice since then. He even attended two of my counseling sessions. We talk at least two times a week and have developed a great friendship.

One of the most important things I've learned is that I'm not alone. Mercedes, McKenzie, MJ, and Antwan are my family, and I am truly blessed to have them in my life.

I no longer want to die. I want to live life to the fullest, embracing all that comes with it. Whether good or bad, I know I will be okay.